WARNING

This book contains sexually explicit scenes and adult language. It may be considered offensive to some readers. This book is for sale to adults ONLY.

* * * * * * * * * * * * * * * * *

Please store your files wisely where they cannot be accessed by underage readers.

Copyright 2015 by Revelry Publishing

All Rights reserved under International and Pan-American Copyright Conventions. By payment of required fees, you have been granted the non-exclusive, non-transferable right to access and read the text of this book. No part of this text may be reproduced, transmitted, downloaded, decompiled, reverse-engineered or stored in or introduced into any information storage and retrieval system, in any form or by any means, whether electronic or mechanical, now known, hereinafter invented, without express written permission of the publisher.

DISCLAIMER

This book is a work of FICTION. It is not to be confused with reality. Neither the author nor the publisher or its associates assume any responsibility for any loss, injury, death or legal consequences resulting from acting on the contents in this book. The characters, incidents and dialogue are drawn from the author's imagination and are not to be construed as real. While reference might be made to actual historical events or existing locations, the names, characters, places and incidents are either products of the author's imagination or are used fictitiously, and any resemblance to actual persons living or dead, business establishments, events or locales is entirely coincidental. Every character in this book is over 18 years of age. The author's opinions are not to be construed as the opinions of the publisher. The material in this book is for entertainment purposes ONLY. Enjoy.

ISBN-13: 978-1987863383
ISBN-10: 1987863380

Other Books by Carla Coxwell:

<u>Torrid Exposure New Adult Romance Series</u>

April is finished with school and ready to build a career. Coming from a well-to-do family, she has decided to reboot her life completely. With family scars too deep to mend, April craves a fresh start. But the past is harder to shake than April ever would have imagined. At the center of it all is Bennett, an old family friend who is the heir to a billionaire media mogul company. Bennett and April haven't been able to stand each other since they were kids. But as the world shifts, the two of them discover the past might be the key to their future.

<u>Devil's Advocate BBW MC New Adult Romance Series</u>

When Kristie comes home from college, the last thing she is expecting is her world to be turned upside down by the appearance of her step-brother, Gray. Gray is rash, impulsive and breaks the law. Kristie's mom asks if she can try to befriend Gray, in hopes to get him on the straight and narrow. The plan backfires, however, as Kristie finds herself falling for Gray. Is it possible he feels the same way? The connection between them threatens to tear down everything Kristie has ever held dear.

<u>Fifty Recipes For Disaster New Adult Romance Series</u>

Trying to win a competition for best chef is cut-throat business. Kiara Sands has just won the opportunity of a lifetime. When she arrives at Fission, she has no idea just how much her life is going to change. She's immediately introduced to Jenny Foster and Robbs Martin, her competitors in the cut throat competition. The only thing Kiara finds more distracting than Robbs' hateful attitude is the handsome executive chef, Paul Weston. It doesn't help matters that Paul is quite taken by Kiara, and showers her with more attention than he gives her competitors.

<u>Star Bright New Adult Romance Series</u>

Torn between her feelings for her agent, Jon, and Rich, a charming bad boy who has ties in the movie industry, Jenny finds herself working through her own past to try to get a grip on her present. As she struggles to learn the lesson that in Hollywood not everyone is what they appear to be, Jenny tries to become a person that she can be proud of. Will she be able to find love and success in Hollywood? Or will she be dragged down by her past forever?

Get the latest update on new releases from the author at:

https://www.carlacoxwell.com/newsletter

This book contains all the stories of the "<u>Obsessed Bounty Hunter Romance Series</u>"

1 - Secrets Revealed

Jacqui Schneider couldn't help it. Every time the memories of her family's brutal murder haunted her, she had to escape. The only thing that could replace her sorrow was sex... and lots of it. And so Jacqui developed a pattern of self-destruction by sleeping with random men that she picked up at a local hotel bar. One day, Uncle Max, an old family friend, appeared. He revealed a secret about her father that would change her life forever.

2 - Heart Surrendered

Jaqui thought the training was tough. But keeping her mind concentrated on her task was even tougher after meeting her new trainer. Adam had a rugged handsome face and ripped abs. She hated that Adam was so demanding. Jacqui's boxing technique was never up to his standards. How can she hate someone so much and yet feel such strong attraction? Was he flirting with her while trying to show her the correct stance? If so, the game of seduction was on.

3 - Rapid Pulse Bounty

With her new skills fully developed, Jacqui was a confident bounty hunter with a few successful captures under her belt. Things were looking up for her. The only thing missing in her life right now was Adam. She hadn't seen him since before her first successful mission. He had left before she could show off her triumph. Jacqui admitted to herself that she was in love with a man who belonged to someone else.

Obsessed Bounty Hunter Romance Series

Books One to Three

By Carla Coxwell

Copyright Revelry Publishing 2015

Table of Contents

Book One – Secrets Revealed

Chapter One

JACQUI SCHNEIDER awoke with a sudden start, the unfamiliarity of her surroundings sending waves of panic sweeping all through her body. Her head whipped frantically from side to side as her eyes swept across the shadowy interior.

She could see the white sheer curtain drawn across the glass window. The sky outside the window had a purplish hue, indicating the first blush of dawn. A console table just below the window held a tray with a thermos bottle and a cup and saucer set neatly stacked beside it. A beige telephone and a digital clock with the time displayed as 4:27 a.m. rested on the other side of the console table. She recognized her clothes as they lay strewn on the floor. Her high-heeled shoes and purse lay in a pile near the door.

She was in a hotel room. As awareness took over, Jacqui was glad her sudden movement did not disturb the sleeping form beside her. She glanced at the figure snoring softly and saw his hand reach out for her. He stirred, breathing deeply, and then resumed his sleep. Jacqui hoped he would not notice the empty space beside him as she tiptoed silently out of bed and gathered her clothes from the floor.

Jacqui wanted to leave the hotel before the man woke up. Things were less complicated that way. She couldn't even remember his name. Was it John… or Jack… or Jim…?

Jacqui didn't really care. It was strictly sexual. She had no intention of ever seeing him again. He was just a random guy she had picked up in the hotel bar last night. The guys were always the same. Non-threatening, married, from out of town, and only out to have a good time. A few made a play of removing their wedding rings. But Jacqui could always spot the telltale lighter skin tone where the ring used to be.

This suited Jacqui just fine. It wasn't a good idea to hook up with someone local. She always made sure the guy was at the hotel for a convention, or just an overnight stay. She usually spotted them because of the name tag pinned over their breast pocket. She'd sit in the bar with her drink, until someone struck up a conversation or offered her a drink.

Jacqui was very hard not to notice. She was tall and lithe and had full breasts, milky white skin, and a nice round ass. She had sparkling green eyes, high cheekbones and luscious lips, topped by chestnut brown hair that fell softly to her shoulders; she attracted instant attention. And this guy…Jim…Jacqui suddenly remembered, was no different. He made a beeline for her as soon as he spotted her at the bar.

"Hi, my name's Jim… I hope you don't mind the intrusion…" Jacqui remembered him saying. "But it looks like your glass needs a refill." Jacqui gave him a smile. It was the standard pickup line. He didn't know she already pegged him through the glass mirrors lining the liquor cabinet of the bar. He was going to be "it" for tonight.

"Are you staying in this hotel?" Jim asked, signaling the bartender for another shot of brandy for her. "No…" Jacqui answered. "Are you waiting for someone…?" Jim asked. Jacqui could read the expectant look in his eyes, and this was usually her cue. If she didn't like what she saw or if she had second thoughts about her safety, she'd say… "Yes, I'm just waiting for my boyfriend to pick me up…" Or offer some other lame excuse.

But she had liked what she saw. Jim was tall, good-looking and neatly dressed. And he had a ring on his finger. "No…" Jacqui answered and gave him a flirty smile. "My name is Nina…" she added. Yes, she would be a horny Nina tonight, or Glenna, or Linda. It didn't really matter. She just wanted to get laid. And tonight, Jim was it.

Jacqui could predict how the next hour would play out. Jim will tell her his life story as he kept filling up her glass hoping to get her drunk enough so she would be pliant when he made his move. The thought almost made Jacqui laugh. The poor guy didn't know that was exactly her plan.

"You've hardly told me anything about yourself, Nina…" Jim complained playfully, as his hand dropped down to her knee. "There's really nothing to tell…I'm just a girl hoping to get lucky tonight…" Jacqui whispered seductively in his ear. His hand moved a little further up her skirt as Jacqui opened her legs a little wider to allow him to feel her crotch through her sheer stockings. Jim's eyes opened wide in surprise as he felt the heat emanating through the silk.

"Why don't we finish this conversation upstairs in my room?" Jim asked. Jacqui nodded her head in reply as her bosom heaved in anticipation. This was the reason she was here tonight. This guy, Jim, would make her forget even for just a few hours, those thoughts and images that constantly lurked in her psyche, tormenting her. When they came uninvited, Jacqui knew what would make her forget. Sex.

Jacqui sashayed her way out of the bar ahead of him. She wanted him to see her firm ass, tapered waist, and long slim legs. It was hard to ignore the looks from other men that followed her and this aroused her even more. She made her way out and straight into the banks of elevators. Jim could hardly contain his excitement. His erection was bulging through his pants.

As soon as the bedroom door closed behind them, Jacqui dropped down on her knees and unzipped his pants. She grabbed hold of his cock. She spit down on it as her hands feverishly stroked it. Jim was hardly out of his pants before Jacqui had him inside her mouth. Jim threw back his head in arousal. He was stunned at the ferocity with which Jacqui moved her head back and forth, her saliva leaving his shaft red and glistening. Jacqui toyed with the head of his cock and tasted the sweet dew that signaled that he would cum prematurely if she didn't slow down.

And Jim didn't want to cum just yet. He had plans of sucking and tasting every inch of her. He would fuck her hard, until the tension building inside his body became unbearable, and then he would blow his load in her mouth. He pulled her up and began to unhook her bra. Jacqui's face was wild with anticipation as she shimmied out of her clothes and stockings. A slight sweat broke out in her armpits. Her boobs swelled as Jim groped one breast with his hand and twirled his thumb and forefinger around the sensitive nipple. Using his mouth, he sucked on the other nipple. Jacqui arched her back in pleasure as waves of ice and fire shot straight through to her groin.

Jim continued sucking her breast and nibbling her nipple with his teeth. His other hand traveled down her flat stomach. He stopped just below her mound, feeling the coarse pubes that covered her vagina. Using his fingers to separate the lips, he caressed her clit and discovered just how wet and aroused she was. Jim stroked her clit repeatedly. He slid in another finger, adding pressure with every stroke. He could feel the inner muscles of her vagina tightening each time his hand brushed against her swollen clitoris. Jacqui closed her eyes and moaned her pleasure. Getting fingered felt really good.

But Jacqui knew she wanted more than his fingers. Pulling him along, she lay back against the bed and opened her thighs. Her pussy was slick with her own juice. "Do you like what you see?" she whispered up at him as Jim nodded. "Eat me. Show me what your tongue can do…" she whispered huskily as she caressed herself to arouse him. Jacqui grabbed her knees and spread her legs even wider for him, leaning her head back against the pillow. Her invitation was obvious, insistent.

Jim scrambled up the bed, his erect penis bouncing with the movement. Then he knelt down between her legs, enthralled with the red-hot pussy before him. He lowered his head as his hands separated the lips of her vagina, exposing the engorged clit. He flicked his tongue against it as Jacqui's body heaved with pleasure. He flicked repeatedly; mesmerized by the guttural sounds emanating from Jacqui's mouth each time his rough tongue made contact with the sensitive skin.

She began to moan as he went faster and faster until finally she couldn't take it anymore. She wanted to feel his cock inside her. Jim positioned himself on top of her. He used his elbows to steady himself as his cock searched for her vagina's opening. Jacqui savored the feeling of the velvety skin of his cock rubbing against the slick wetness of her clit. Jim rammed himself inside her. And then he drew back until the head of his cock was barely past the opening of her vaginal wall. Then he rammed into her once again, filling her completely.

Jacqui flattened her heels against the hard muscle of Jim's buttocks, urging him to go faster and faster. She needed him to fuck her hard. It was what drove the demons away. Every thrust made her moan louder and louder. Her pussy was on fire. Tension swept all over her body and gathered within her groin. Unexpectedly, Jim flipped her over. Jacqui buried her face into the pillow. With her ass in the air, he entered her from behind. His hands reached out and groped her nipples. The sensation of his fingers pinching and pulling her nipple while ramming her pussy was too much to bear. She knew she couldn't hold on much longer. She hoped that Jim was nearly there.

"I'm coming…" Jim grunted in her ear. The words were like fuel that ignited the raging fire from within. She gave in to a powerful orgasm that shook her body as she felt Jim shudder repeatedly behind her. After a couple of seconds, Jim lowered her gently on the bed as he withdrew from her and spooned her from behind. Jacqui got what she had come for. She was exhausted. She closed her eyes as languid exhaustion filled her completely. Sleep came within seconds. A dreamless sleep that held at bay all the horrors that she wanted to forget.

Chapter Two

Jacqui slid the key into the lock of her single storey house. The whole neighborhood was silent. She was glad no one was around to see her. She didn't need that kind of talk, especially since….

She glanced at the houses lining the street where she lived. Tall sycamore trees lined the sidewalk like silent sentinels. A child's red bike leaned haphazardly by the fence railing in one of the houses. A neighbor had left his garden sprinkler on and the water spray hitting the sunlight created a rainbow as it arced across the yard. Three houses down from hers, a teenaged boy riding his bike threw a newspaper that landed on the grass near the porch. A dog could be heard barking in the distance. It was a neighborhood that resembled myriad others all across America.

Jacqui sighed deeply. She was envious of her neighbors. Every night she imagined what it was like to be inside those homes. The warmth of sleeping bodies as they lay in bed, tucked warmly, cozy within the loving embrace of loved ones. Safe and secure.

Except for Jacqui. She hated coming home. And her front yard showed it. Tall weeds and grass covered the yard, badly in need of a trim. Her porch was littered with unread newspapers dating back to three months ago. She had paid the newspaper boy weeks ago and told him to stop coming. But she had never bothered to put away the dailies that now littered her porch. She was afraid to open them. She knew the headlines would just bring her back to those terrifying days.

Of course, she could hire someone to clean up for her. Guilty feelings assailed her because it didn't use to be this way. She felt embarrassed. But her neighbors seemed to understand. At least no one had complained yet. They were giving her time, she thought. The interior of the house wasn't so bad except for the accumulation of dust everywhere. Curtains permanently drawn against the windows allowed for very little sunlight as they hung listlessly against the glass panes. But for Jacqui it was a blessing. She didn't need to see the living room where it had all happened.

She tried calling Mrs. Evans once on the off-chance that she would agree to clean up for her. But instinctively, she knew the cleaning lady would say no. Jacqui couldn't really blame her. So she left things the way they were three months ago. The Crime Scene Clean-up Crew did a good job of removing the bloodstains. Jacqui was grateful for that. She avoided entering the dark living room or using the kitchen. But dust had a way of seeping through cracks in the floor and had accumulated everywhere. Jacqui didn't have the will to do anything about it.

Her footsteps echoed across the floor of the empty house as she walked toward her bedroom at the end of the hallway. She pushed open the bedroom door not even bothering to switch on the lights. What for? She knew her way around. Her room was her solace. The familiarity was comforting.

Right now, all she wanted was to take her clothes off and jump into the shower. Thank God she had her own bathroom. One of the perks her parents had gifted her when she decided to stay instead of getting her own place. She would report for work late today, she decided.

Her boss understood her situation and allowed her to come in anytime she wanted to. Heck, he even insisted she take a vacation and reassured her she would still have a job when she got back. Jacqui was grateful but adamant. She needed to fill the hours of her day. That… and she needed the money to survive.

Because of the darkness that surrounded her, Jacqui failed to see the figure watching her silently from the wingback chair pushed carelessly against the wall.

"Hello Jacqui…" the voice greeted her. Jacqui wheeled around in fright, her heart pounding wildly. The figure stood slowly and made its way to the light switch. "Uncle Max…? What…where…oh my God you scared me to death…" Jacqui stammered. She wanted to run to him and hug him. He was a familiar figure. A comforting presence. Someone she had known since she was a child. But suddenly, anger replaced the joy she felt in seeing Uncle Max again.

"What are you doing here?" she asked icily. "I came to see how you were doing," Uncle Max replied with calmness, so typical of the way Jacqui remembered him. "You came to see how I…?" Jacqui repeated as her anger turned to fury. "You didn't even come to their funeral. You were my dad's best friend. How could you do that? I called so many times but your phone was disconnected," Jacqui wailed. Tears of anger and frustration welled up in her eyes. "I couldn't, Jacqui...I couldn't afford for the Police and the FBI to make the connection," Uncle Max explained.

"Connection...? What are you talking about?" Jacqui demanded in an accusing voice. Uncle Max drew a deep breath and replied, "Jac, there are a lot of things you don't know. But believe me when I say that staying away... not saying goodbye for the last time...that was the hardest thing I ever did." Jacqui saw Uncle Max struggling to keep his emotions in check. Suddenly all the pent-up tears came rushing out. The intensity caught Jacqui by surprise and knocked the air out of her. Jacqui swayed as Uncle Max reached out to catch her. He held her tenderly as her silent tears gave way to heavy sobs which still did not manage to ease the pain that racked her heart. Incoherent words spewed from her lips as she relived the incident.

"It was frightening... I was in my room when I heard dad pleading to spare my mom... He was using his body to shield her. Mom was crying hysterically... struggling to get in front of my dad as if to shield him," Jacqui's voice cracked as she remembered. Then she continued, "The man had the gun pointed at his head... the gunshot was so silent. I didn't even realize he had fired. At first I thought it was my dad that got hit. But then I saw my mom topple over as dad screamed." A fresh wave of sobs made her voice incoherent. But Jacqui couldn't stop.

"Dad cradled my mom as she lay on the floor with a surprised look on her face. Then she reached out and touched dad's face. Dad just kept saying no...no...no...The killer did it on purpose, Uncle Max.

He wanted my dad to see him murder my mom. And then…and then… Danny appeared from the kitchen. He still held a spoon in his hand. He was eating cereal. Uncle Max, I didn't even know my brother was home. I thought he was still in school. But he must have gotten sick and mom made him stay home. Then the man wheeled around and shot him too. He was just a kid…he was just a little boy."

The old man's shirt was drenched with her tears as the memory sent shockwaves of pain, remembering the bloody slaughter. Then Jacqui continued on, "My dad screamed with rage. Then he tried to grab the gun away. The man shot him in the head. He didn't even see me crouching behind the door. I wanted to scream for help, but I was frozen with terror. I couldn't move. Everything happened so fast. It felt like hours before I realized the man was gone. I crawled all the way to see them. There was blood everywhere. I didn't know I was screaming until the neighbors came."

Jacqui finally allowed months of pent up feeling to come out as she bawled and screeched her sorrow over the tragic murder of her family. Uncle Max held her gently, tenderly, allowing her tears to lighten the load she had carried all these months. After what seemed like an eternity, Jacqui's heaves eventually settled into quiet sobs, and then to silent sniffles, until she just lay exhausted in his arms.

"It's alright, baby girl, everything will be alright…" Uncle Max consoled her. Jacqui looked up and smiled into his face and said, "I'm glad you're here now." Uncle Max held her at arm's length and said, "We need to talk, Jac. Can we do that? There are things you need to know. Go take a shower. Change your clothes and come with me. There's an all-night café near the park where we can chat."

Jacqui nodded her head in agreement. She entered the bathroom, took a quick shower, and came out with a towel wrapped around her body. She rummaged through her closet for some clean clothes. "Aren't you going to give me some privacy while I change?" she asked. Uncle Max was relieved to hear the hint of amusement in her voice.

"I've changed your diapers since you were a baby. You've got nothing that I haven't seen," Uncle Max replied seriously. Jacqui smiled, took a pair of jeans and a light cashmere sweater and reentered the bathroom. In a couple of minutes she was out again, with her hair tied back into a ponytail. She was eager to hear what Uncle Max had to say. Maybe he had some ideas that could help the FBI and the Police. They had drawn a blank and the case had been shelved until a new lead could be found.

Uncle Max led the way out of her bedroom. Instead of going straight for the door, he walked into the living room and stood near the spot where her mom and dad and Danny died. He stood still except when he wiped away the tears from his eyes. And then he walked towards Jacqui and ushered her out the door. They strolled down two blocks and turned a corner where he approached a car that was parked by the sidewalk. Jacqui understood that he didn't want the neighbors to see him. Suddenly she realized there was so much she did not know about Uncle Max. Dad said they were together in the military until both were discharged. But even her dad didn't talk much about the past.

Uncle Max was a familiar figure that had come to visit through the years. A doting man they learned to call Uncle. He would stay for a couple of days here and there, and during those times, Jacqui remembered how happy his dad seemed to have him around. They would often talk in his study for hours. Her mom showered him with affection and treated him sweetly. Jacqui had always assumed he was a distant relative.

Still, Jacqui couldn't remember any stories about where he lived or if Uncle Max had family somewhere. It dawned on Jacqui that Uncle Max was the closest person to a family that she had. The thought left her feeling sad, but somehow at ease. At least for now he was here.

Chapter Three

Jacqui stared incredulously at the old man seated in front of her. Two empty mugs of coffee and a plate of sandwiches were the only witnesses to everything Uncle Max had said. He spoke in a low voice, eyes alert and constantly looking around. He would stop whenever someone came within earshot.

Jacqui felt her head would explode. She was stunned. She didn't know what to say. "I understand it's a bit much to take in all at once…" the old man said, seeing the bewilderment on her face. "A bit much? How about me realizing I didn't really know my dad after all these years. He was just…dad," Jacqui replied still in denial.

And then she continued in amazement, "My dad was a bounty hunter?" "Yup, one of the best. I recruited him and trained him," Uncle Max replied. The old man continued, "During the times he was away from you guys, he was out there tracking someone." Jacqui remembered the long absences from home. But mom always said dad had a job as a consulting engineer building bridges or making roads somewhere. Jacqui learned to accept it. Whenever he came home he was always exhausted and seemed to have lost weight. Jacqui concluded it was because he had worked very hard during his travels. But he always had presents for her and Danny. A token from one of the many places where he worked, he said.

And whenever he was around, he brought them everywhere - the mall, the dentist, to the doctor's office. He drove them to school every single day. He even cooked breakfast for them. He often joked he was giving mom a rest from all these chores because he was away a lot. And mom seemed like a changed woman whenever dad came home. She would smile more often unlike when he was away. She was always tense and irritable. Her mom was totally devoted to her dad.

Growing up, Jacqui had looked forward to his return every time he went away. Dad was cool and easygoing. He allowed them liberties while mom would just shake her head in disapproval. Now, she suddenly realized he was making up for his absences, grateful perhaps, that he had made it home safe and in one piece.

"Did mom know about his other job…his real job?" Jacqui asked. "Yes, your mom knew about it," Uncle Max replied. Jacqui whistled through her teeth. So it wasn't a secret. Her mom must have supported her dad all the way. Jacqui stared at her Uncle Max once again. She wouldn't have such a hard time accepting him as the bounty hunter, but not her dad. Uncle Max was tall and burly. Even at his age, almost 70 years old, Jacqui believed he could beat the shit out of any younger guy.

But remembering her dad, Jacqui found it hard to think so. Dad was never violent. He was shorter than Uncle Max, and wasn't the athletic type. Jacqui never saw him exercise or lift weights or do stuff that required much strength. "Shouldn't a bounty hunter be some kind of macho man, with bulging muscles… someone who can kick ass?" Jacqui inquired, still unable to go from the picture of the dad she knew to the man her Uncle Max spoke about.

"Jac, being a bounty hunter doesn't have anything to do with muscles or being the strongest man alive," Uncle Max informed her. "Your dad was one of the best because he had a sharp mind that he camouflaged by being ordinary. He could blend well in a crowd and not look suspicious. That was his strength. You'd be surprised how many fugitives we managed to capture because they thought he was just another guy they could push around. He wasn't intimidating to anyone," Uncle Max explained.

"But how did he protect himself when things went bad? I assume he must have had some sticky situations," Jacqui asked curiously. The old man gave this some thought before he replied. "Your dad was a dead shot with a firearm. He was a sharpshooter. He could take down anyone from fifty meters away. And besides, he said he was the fastest thing on foot when he needed to be."

Jacqui laughed at that. She did remember her dad running after a pickpocket who had snatched her mom's purse near the mall. He overtook the younger guy and tackled him to the ground. This also explained his one passion. He loved guns. He had a collection, but he always kept them under lock and key because of Danny. But it was also through a gun that he had lost his life, and her mom's and Danny's too.

Uncle Max saw the sudden change in her expression and knew she was remembering that fatal day once again. He reached out his hand and clasped hers from across the table. "Jac, your dad left you some money. I want you to know that. You never need to work again or worry about your future as long as you decide to live simply." Jacqui looked up in surprise. She hadn't seen that coming.

"Your dad never touched a single cent of what he earned as a bounty hunter. And he earned a lot. He placed it all in a trust fund for you and Danny. He called it his 'what if something happens to me' money. But with Danny gone, it's all yours now. I hope you don't mind that I invested it in some bonds. Your dad agreed it was the best thing," Uncle Max said.

"How much money did he leave for me and Danny?" Jacqui was curious to know. "Here's the information on the accounts. The money is yours anytime you want," Uncle Max said, handing her a memory stick and a number scribbled on a piece of paper. Jacqui almost choked on the amount. She kept silent, her mind reeling over everything she just learned.

She looked all around her. The café was slowly filling up with early morning patrons ordering coffee on their way to work. Everything looked so ordinary. And yet it wasn't. She was now all alone in the world without a family to share her failures, her triumphs, or her plans for the future. She also happened to be rich because of the money dad had left her.

This made her think about her future plans. What was there for her to do? She was 24 years old and until three months ago, she was still living at home with her mom and dad. But that was because her mom had needed help to look after Danny whenever dad was away. But now they were all gone.

"Hmm….Bounty Hunter…" she murmured softly to herself. It sounded like something straight from a B movie. And she had lived with one for 24 years without knowing it. Suddenly she remembered something very important. "Uncle Max, was my family murdered because of this…this bounty hunter stuff?" Jacqui asked.

Uncle Max drew a sigh before he replied, "I believe so. Your dad was on the trail of a notorious arms dealer. He was posing as a supplier. He managed to set a meeting with the target. But the guy never showed. We concluded that your dad's cover was blown… perhaps the target acquired fresh information about who your dad really was."

"These guys are vicious, Jac. Vengeance is a common occurrence. It's a way of sending the message, 'you don't mess with us.' Your dad knew that. He lived knowing each job could be his last," the old man said. "Who's the guy, Uncle Max?" Jacqui asked curiously. She had an instinct that the old man knew something. Uncle Max sighed deeply. A troubled look marked his face.

He looked Jacqui in the eye and replied, "Jac, in my line of business there is information that is too sensitive to disclose. I can't tell you that. I have no proof and I answer to a higher authority. All we do is supply the name and whereabouts of the person we track. We get paid big money for that information. When one of us gets killed, everything connecting us to that person is erased. That's why you couldn't get in touch with me after your family was murdered."

Jacqui could hardly believe Uncle Max wasn't going to help her catch her family's killer. Yet a quiet acceptance started to dawn on her. Her dad had done this for a living. She had to respect that. He had known the risks he was taking and he prepared to face them. Her dad loved them so much, and had wanted to guarantee a good future for her and Danny. She was sure of that.

Uncle Max stood up. Jacqui knew this conversation was over and followed him out the door of the café. The old man thought it was best to go while he still had the will to keep silent. It would not do any good to let on more than Jacqui needed to know. Both were silent on the drive back home.

"You're leaving again," Jacqui said as Uncle Max reached the driveway to her house. She hoped he could stay longer, although she noticed there was no luggage to indicate a longer visit. "Yes, baby girl…" Uncle Max replied as he searched for something in the backseat of the car.

His hand drew out a cell phone, which he handed to Jacqui. Jacqui looked at it curiously. "Call me if you need anything. Use this… but only to call me. No one should know about this phone. Hide it. Is that understood?" Uncle Max asked. Jacqui nodded her head, acknowledging that she understood. She tucked the phone into the pocket of her pants and stepped out of the car.

"I love you, Uncle Max," Jacqui said through the window. "Love you too, baby girl," Uncle Max replied before driving away, glancing at the receding figure of Jacqui through the rearview mirror. Jacqui stepped into the threshold of the house, caressing the phone that bulged through the pocket of her pants. She walked into the living room and drew the curtains aside to let the sunshine in.

As light flooded into the room, Jacqui felt less lonely for the first time in a long time. Things will change, she thought. It will become easier in time. She just needed to find out what she wanted to do with her life. She could make a phone call. She had a lifeline.

Chapter Four

Whistling a happy tune in her head, Jacqui surveyed her front yard. The grass, which had grown wild and untended the last couple of weeks, was trimmed and a gardener had spread soil along the path leading to the house. Jacqui had bought flowering plants, hoping the bloom would make the house feel homier.

A long time neighbor, Mrs. Higgins waved at her and then decided to come over for a chat. "Hello, Jacqui…" the old lady greeted her, holding tightly to the leash of her Boston terrier, Checkers. "Hi Mrs. Higgins," Jacqui answered happily, glad for the company. She knelt down and gave Checkers a scratch behind the ears.

"I see you're putting in some flowers," Mrs. Higgins smiled, "Nothing like a bunch of flowers to make one feel happy." "Yup," Jacqui agreed as she squirmed away from the dog, who was intent on licking her face. An awkward silence followed. Jacqui knew Mrs. Higgins wanted to give her some consoling words but was hesitant to talk about it.

"It was a horrible tragedy…I'm so sorry for you…" Mrs. Higgins managed to say. "I'm sorry too, Jacqui replied, "but things are getting better now." "Take all the time you need, Honey. It was a horrible thing that you went through. I don't know what's happening in the world. Right in your own home…" Mrs. Higgins muttered, shaking her head in disbelief.

Jacqui thanked the old lady and walked back to sit down by the porch steps. She was feeling better. Uncle Max's short visit a couple of days ago must have triggered something inside her brain. She had called her employer right after he left and asked if the offer for a vacation was still on. Her boss was more than glad to give it to her.

Jacqui had asked for two weeks leave. She then searched the yellow pages for a cleaning lady from out of town. She reckoned the woman wouldn't be as concerned that a murder had taken place right in her own home. But the service did request for higher rates coming from out of town.

Jacqui was more than glad to pay it. The cleaning lady had arrived the very next morning and stayed until everything was shiny and clean. They changed the curtains and removed the dusty covers from the throw pillows in the living room. The living room floors were waxed and vacuumed, and the linoleum kitchen floors polished until they shone.

For the first time in three months, Jacqui had entered her parents' bedroom. Everything was as it was on the night they were killed. Jacqui managed to put away her mom and dad's clothes in boxes to be picked up by a Goodwill truck. She was surprised by how very little personal stuff her father owned. There were no legal documents except the deed to the house, which Jacqui planned on securing in a safety deposit box.

Her mom was never much into fashion or make-up, never favored jewelry, and simply relied on an old wristwatch for an accessory. Jacqui fingered the watch and decided to keep it as a memento. When she entered Danny's room, Jacqui was suddenly assailed with a vicious loneliness. If her mom and dad had lived simply, Danny's room was filled with toys that could make a little boy very happy. His Play Station Portable 3000 rested on the bed, while a stack of DVD's of his favorite cartoons lay scattered on the floor.

Danny was prone to asthma attacks. Dad and mom made sure he was happy inside his room during those days he couldn't go out. That must have been why he was at home instead of in school during that fateful day. The thought brought sudden tears to Jacqui's eyes, which she brusquely brushed away. She didn't want the cleaning lady see her lose it. Happy over the clean house, Jacqui cooked some eggs smothered in cheese and brought it to the living room. She flicked on the TV and leaned back against the soft cushions. With the cleaning lady gone, she had the whole house to herself.

The soft drone of the television set was hypnotic. Exhaustion crept in. An exhausted Jacqui succumbed to the temptation and closed her eyes. She had probably fallen asleep when she felt a cold object press against her temple. Jacqui's eyes flew open. A dark figure stood beside her with a gun pointed into her face. Jacqui cringed in terror.

"We never leave unsettled business behind," the man said in a cold and cruel voice. Then he continued with a sneer, "It was a pleasure seeing your daddy scream when I shot your mom. His rage when I killed your little brother almost gave me an orgasm. Too bad, he won't see me do the same thing to you know now."

Jacqui screamed as a loud crash deafened her. She bolted upright and flailed her hands to defend herself. That's when she saw her uneaten plate of eggs littered on the floor. Broken pieces of plate glass scattered everywhere. The crash must have been what awakened her. She was all alone in the house.

Realizing she had a nightmare, Jacqui buried her face in her hands, crying softly. The house suffocated her. She couldn't breathe. The images of her family's slaughter played like a movie reel in her mind, torturing her. Foolishly she thought that she already had it under control.

A growing heat in her groin signaled what she desired most at this time. She needed to get laid again. It was the remedy her body craved for. Like an addict seeking an escape from reality, Jacqui entered her bedroom, took a quick shower, and rummaged through her closet.

Taking out a little black dress matched with pointy high-heeled shoes and a set of lace undies, Jacqui dressed hurriedly. She hoped to God there was a convention somewhere where she could find another random guy.

Brushing her hair vigorously until it shone and curled softly against her shoulder, Jacqui grabbed hold of a red lipstick. She moved closer to the mirror and stared at her eyes reflecting back at her. Is this really what you want to do, Jacqui? How long will you play this dangerous game before you get into trouble or catch some kind of disease? What if the next random guy turns out to be a creep and beats you up? Then what? Everything your dad worked for and died for is meaningless. Your dad was a hero. Every bad element he helped put away makes this world safer for others. And how do you honor your family's memory? By being a slut.

Jacqui stared at her own reflection for a long time. An idea was slowly forming in her head. An idea that could be the answer to the question she often asked herself these past few days. What do I really want to do with my life? Where do I go from here?

She had no boyfriend. No other family to make a connection with. She had lots of acquaintances at the office where she worked, but no close friends. She would be perfect for what she had in mind, because her absence wouldn't be noticed. She could train and be prepared to face the challenges. Yes, it seemed everything that had happened these last few months had led her toward the major decision that was slowly taking place inside her head.

And then a thought struck her. What if she came face to face with the murderer of her family? Would she recognize him? Everything that had happened that particular night was a blur in her memory. Instinctively, she knew she would recognize him when she saw him again. That kind of tragedy left its mark on the brain. Something about the way he had moved, perhaps? Jacqui wasn't sure how, but she vowed she would avenge her family someday.

As these thoughts crossed her mind, Jacqui noticed that she no longer felt the need to fuck someone. The urgent heat dissipated between her legs. In place of the sudden sexual pleasure her body craved, she felt determined. A steely resolve took control of her entire body.

She walked to the drawer and rummaged through the clothes within. Thrusting her arm deep within the recesses, her hand groped for a drawstring pouch that held a familiar object. Pulling the cloth bag out of its hiding place, Jacqui slid the string open and removed the cell phone within. She pressed the call button and heard the phone make a connection before it started ringing.

Jacqui waited with bated breath as the phone rang incessantly somewhere. She closed her eyes and hoped Uncle Max would pick up. Finally after what seemed like an eternity, she heard the click that signaled that the phone was now live in someone's hand.

"Hello…hello..." Jacqui spoke into the phone. There was only silence at the end of the open line. Jacqui instinctively knew her Uncle Max was there, listening. Without much ado, Jacqui stated her purpose.

"Uncle Max I know you can hear me. I've made a decision. You may not agree with me but if not with you, I'll go look for someone else who will take me in. Uncle Max, I've decided I want to be a bounty hunter too. Just like my daddy."

Jacqui didn't hear any reply. Only white noise filled the air before the phone was disconnected from the other end. But Jacqui wasn't worried. She knew Uncle Max had heard all she had to say. She took off her little black dress with a smirk on her face. She had no more use for it tonight. She kicked off her high-heels and removed all traces of make-up from her face before slipping on her pajamas.

She stepped out of her room and walked through the whole house, turning off the lights behind her as she passed through each room. She was no longer afraid.

There was a serene calmness in her face that hadn't been there before. This was the answer to her questions around why her family was killed. She believed everything happened for a purpose, and she had discovered her true purpose. Just like her dad before her, she would make this world a safer place for others. The thought made her smile.

Jacqui knew she could kick ass if she needed to.

-To be continued in Book 2-

Book Two – Heart Surrendered

Chapter One

JACQUI CHUGGED the water from the container like a thirsty beast. She just couldn't get enough of it. 'Water never tasted so good, better than an orgasm,' Jacqui thought, as she splashed some straight into her face. Jacqui was parched, grimy, and her body ached like she just went through a meat grinder. She was up at 0400 hours in her jogging suit and trainers. Uncle Max met her at the door of a building that resembled a huge hangar.

When Uncle Max said yesterday that training started today before the crack of dawn, Jacqui thought he meant some light exercises that would involve sit-ups and jumping jacks. She was never further from the truth. The next couple of hours had been the most intensive Jacqui ever subjected her body to. And she knew this was just the start.

Uncle Max led her through a routine of squats and crunches, lunges and hamstring curls until her ass had no more feeling left in them. "C'mon Jacqui, move that body," Uncle Max shouted like a drill sergeant. Then he moved on to pull ups, sit-ups, bicep curls, and the bench press. Her arms and legs felt disconnected from her body. Her hand was shaking so hard she almost dropped the water bottle she was holding. She was grateful for the fifteen minute break the old man gave her.

"Alright, Jacqui… back to work…" Uncle Max shouted from the sidelines. She wanted to complain but didn't have the courage to. When she arrived yesterday, Uncle Max told her exactly what to expect for the next couple of weeks. He was dead serious as he went through the program with her. If he was trying to discourage her, he almost succeeded. But Jacqui was too proud to say it. She had come this far to become a bounty hunter.

Before she even got settled into the cot that would be hers during her stay, Uncle Max talked to her privately in what he called his 'interrogation room.' It was a small building at the back of the property. The walls were lined with an assortment of maps indicating the different states of the United States. There were yellow pins tacked on certain cities within the map. Jacqui looked around curiously. She noticed the different surveillance gadgets like GPS tracking, high resolution cameras, night vision goggles, an assortment of pens, and spy gear which she was seeing for the first time in her life.

A bank of television sets was stacked near the wall manned by a single individual. Jacqui saw it was streaming live from some part of the country she did not recognize. A huge glass cabinet held an assortment of guns, some she recognized from her dad's own collection.

"Take a seat Jacqui," Uncle Max indicated a wooden table with hardback chairs in a small corner of the room. He did not speak for some time and Jacqui had a strong desire to squirm under his intense gaze.

"Are you sure this is what you want because right now I am here to tell you, it's not going to be an easy life," Uncle Max said. Jacqui nodded her head, indicating she understood. When she came to her decision back home on the night she called Uncle Max, she quit her job the very next day. She told her boss she wanted to do some travelling. Her boss gave her the go-signal. "It's probably what you need right now," he even said.

Jacqui wasn't sure what Uncle Max thought about the whole idea. She hadn't heard from him since she made the call. But a few days later she found an envelope that was left on her porch. There was no forwarding address and it didn't look like it came by mail. Inside was a one-way ticket to Utah and strict instructions what to bring along. Only a small backpack was needed for the clothing list. It became pretty obvious this was not going to be some luxurious holiday.

She was met at the airport by a burly, bald-headed man, wearing dark sunglasses on a stern face. He reminded Jacqui of an ex-marine or military man. He ushered her into a waiting SUV, got behind the wheel, and started the engine.

They left the city behind until all Jacqui could see were tall mountain ranges in the distance. A few miles onward, they turned into a small dirt road and followed a winding path until Jacqui noticed a copse of large evergreen trees where they seemed to be headed. The trees covered a large expanse of land, save for small clearings with structures that resembled warehouses or large barns. They drove past these until they came to a smaller building where she saw Uncle Max waiting by the door. He greeted her warmly, but Jacqui sensed a certain formality in his demeanor.

Looking at him now, sitting behind the table with a grim expression on his face, Jacqui was suddenly filled with an overwhelming insecurity. Did she make the right decision after all? But Jacqui remembered the downward spiral she was on. The sex with random guys. The orgasms she needed to get some sleep so she could stop thinking about the tragic events of her life. And she needed a purpose… to find some meaning in her life. To honor her dad's memory so she would never forget. For her mom who supported him all the way, and for Danny, who was never given the chance to experience what life was all about.

"Yes, Uncle Max. I have never been surer about anything in my life," she declared with a certain degree of conviction. Uncle Max smiled, and for the first time since she arrived, Jacqui felt relieved. She knew whatever lay ahead, Uncle Max wouldn't spare her, wouldn't try to make things easy for her. She knew that.

"Ok then, let's get you started. I am *The Agency*. I will be responsible for your training. You will not question my decisions… you will do as I say. The training will be rigorous because you will meet all kinds of low-life scumbags. A lot of times your life will be in danger. But you will be trained in self-defense and handling weapons until I feel that you are totally capable of protecting yourself out there. Then and only then will I send you out on a mission. Is that clear?" Uncle Max asked. Jacqui nodded her head in agreement.

"Alright, settle in. You will be shown to your room. Tomorrow your training starts. And for the next couple of days you will only remember pain," The old man warned her. He wasn't kidding. After five hours of the most intense exercise routines she had ever done, Jacqui couldn't even remember her name. Her body hurt even in places she didn't know existed. And this was just her first day in boot camp.

Lunch had been sparse, with just some fish and vegetables. She was given an hour to rest inside her room which was composed of a bunk bed and a footlocker for her personal stuff. No TV, no telephone, no computer or laptop. Then she was called back again and told to run around a circuit she didn't even notice earlier in the day. She tried counting in her head the number of times she completed a circuit before fatigue settled in and lost count completely. It took all her will power to put one leg in front of the other. By the time Uncle Max called for a halt, dusk had settled and stars appeared brightly in a cloudless sky.

"Supper will be brought to your room. Tomorrow we do the whole routine again," Uncle Max declared before he left. It wasn't a request. It was an order. Jacqui trudged slowly back to her room. There is no time to dwell on the unfamiliarity and sparse surroundings. The bed was a most welcome sight and calling her name. She groaned in pain as she stretched her arms over her head to remove her workout clothes. Her back was racked with pain as she bent to unlace her trainers.

Jacqui managed to splash some water onto her face before falling face down into the soft covers with only her undies on. Sleep came easy for Jacqui that night. A sleep so deep she hardly noticed the appearance of two figures in her room.

"You think she'll make it?" an older voice inquired. "I don't know Uncle Max. You put her through the wringer today," the other replied. Uncle Max sighed as he looked at the sleeping form of the girl on the bed. "You're hoping maybe she'll give up and just go back home?" the second figure asked curiously.

"Yes… this kind of life isn't for her. She's been through a lot already. But I also can't accept throwing her life away with all those men in strange hotel rooms," Uncle Max replied. "Well… you said the same thing about me too, remember? I didn't turn out too badly," the younger man said. "No, Adam, you are doing very well. The fact is… you will play an important role in this girl's future," Uncle Max replied.

"I can hardly wait…" Adam replied, taking in the full breasts and rounded ass of the sleeping form on the bed. "Just learn to keep that cock of yours inside your pants…" warned the old man, with a hint of indulgence in his voice.

The two figures departed slowly out of the room where Jacqui Schneider slept an exhausted, dreamless sleep.

Chapter Two

For the next couple of days, Jacqui endured the rigors of her routine with Uncle Max. Although her body was taking a brutal beating, Jacqui realized her mind was getting sharper. Because she slept soundlessly every night, she woke up with muscles still hurting from the day before, but her mind was ready to defy all obstacles the old man managed to put in her face. Uncle Max varied the routine so she got a surprise every time. He said she shouldn't get too satisfied over her progress. They still had a lot of ground to cover.

Although she trained alone with the old man, Jacqui realized the place wasn't as empty as she thought. She noticed some activities going on inside the other buildings. Sometimes she would hear voices but they were always too far away for Jacqui to hear clearly. Once she heard a steady stream of gunshots, which made her freeze in the midst of her routine.

Uncle Max saw her reaction and quickly informed her it was coming from the firing range nearby. He never introduced her to anyone and Jacqui never questioned him. She went through her training with much enthusiasm, never once forgetting the reason she was here.

On the morning of her second week, Jacqui jogged to the building, ready for her daily workout. She never arrived earlier than Uncle Max although she always woke up before the crack of dawn. Same as always, Uncle Max was there waiting for her.

"Morning Jacqui… come walk with me …" the old man said turning towards a path behind the building where they trained every day. "Morning Uncle Max," Jacqui replied, surprised by the sudden change in their daily ritual. "I thought it would be good if we changed our routine today…" her mentor informed her.

The path took a circuitous route among the trees until they arrived in front of a smaller structure. Uncle Max opened the door. Jacqui immediately saw a boxing ring in the center of the huge cavernous room. Grey metal lockers lined one wall. A couple of sand-filled punching bags hung from the ceiling. The room was lit with a few bulbs from the ceiling, casting shadows on the bags where the light hit them. The rest of the room was dark.

"Check the lockers," Uncle Max said, "there are some training shorts and boxing shoes that should fit you." Jacquie did as she was told and found a black pair, perfectly her size. Spotting a new pair of shorts and razor back shirt still in its packaging, Jacqui removed her clothes in a nearby cubicle and donned the new pair.

Entering the room once more, Uncle Max handed Jacqui some headgear and punch mitts. "Just that…? No gloves…? Jacqui asks amusedly. She was expecting heavyweight gloves instead of tiny mitts. "I was thinking we'd start slow," Uncle Max replied. "Boxing is not as easy as it seems." "Uncle Max, I'll finally get to kick some ass…" Jacqui answered gleefully.

"Not until you give me five hundred with this jump rope," a voice cut in from the darkness. Jacqui whirled around in the direction where the voice came from. From out of the dark shadows a man emerged. He was tall and wiry, lean muscles packed tightly over his sun burnt skin. He was wearing loose drawstring pants that hung ridiculously low over his hips. He was barefoot. But what attracted Jacqui's attention was his face. He had the face of an angel similar to those old paintings one would see in museums.

Jacqui stared, mesmerized as he approached. Then she noticed the chiseled face, the blue eyes which stared back at her with scorn, the sharp nose and full lips that were curled in a half-smile. Longish brown hair, badly in need of a trim, was tied at the back of the nape although some curls managed to escape and formed a halo across his face.

"I see you finally got here…Jacqui, meet Adam. Adam, Jacqui," the old man said by means of introduction. Jacqui didn't know where her tongue went. It probably retracted to the back of her open mouth. Stunning…beautiful…sexy… were some of the words running through her befuddled brain. And she was starting to feel gauche and foolish for staring…with an open mouth. Like a robot, she held out her hand for a handshake instead.

Adam reached out for her outstretched hand but instead of shaking it, he removed the mitts, making her feel very foolish…again. "You won't need these for now," he said quietly, taking the other mitt as well, and handing her the jump rope. Jacqui stared at the jump rope like she had never seen one before. She was glad for the distraction as it gave her a little time to regain whatever was left of her shattered composure.

"Don't worry," Uncle Max reassured her, "he has that same effect on all women. It'll pass. As soon as they find out he's an asshole." Adam let out a loud laugh. Uncle Max turned to leave, sending Jacqui to a panic. "You're leaving, Uncle Max?" Jacqui asked stupidly. "You're in good hands and I have some work to catch up on," Uncle Max replied before closing the door behind him.

An awkward silence ensued as Jacqui stood with a rope dangling from her fingers. Adam looked at her sardonically with one eyebrow tilted upward and said, "Well…do you intend to stand there the whole day? I have better things to do than just babysit for the old man."

"What is his problem?" Jacqui thought to herself. Adam moved toward the edge of the boxing ring, slumped lazily against a post with arms akimbo, urging her to start. Jacqui grabbed hold of the handles on each end and swung the rope over her head. Her first few tries were unsuccessful, making her stumble awkwardly.

Adam's laughter didn't help in any way. Jacqui felt a growing irritation in her stomach as she tried again. She finally got the rhythm and managed to jump, counting softly as she went along. "You did say five hundred…?" Jacqui asked out loud. Jacqui discovered that jumping and talking out loud wasn't such an easy thing to do and stumbled once again.

"Start over…" Adam ordered her from the sidelines. "What?" Jacqui asked, irritated. She had managed almost half when she stumbled. "Are you deaf? Start over…" Adam mocked from where he sat at the edge of the ring swinging his feet. Jacqui started over again as the irritation in her stomach turned to slow anger. She needed to focus her mind. She can do this. She just needed to take her mind off the sexy stranger slowly turning into a tyrant in her mind.

She wished she had known beforehand she would be doing jump rope. She would have worn a stronger support bra instead of the regular training bra she had on. She knew her breasts were heaving with her heavy breathing and her nipples were straining hard through the thin layer of the razorback shirt. Mercifully she got to five hundred and dropped the ropes to the ground. She had no intention of going over that again today.

Adam handed her the mitts and led her to the sand filled punching bag. "Let's see what those hands can do…" he said in a taunting voice. Jacqui gave a wordless answer in her head, "Stroke your cock till your eyes pop out…" But she packed a wallop that sent the bag flying. "Not bad…" observed Adam, "but your stance needs improvement."

Adam moved behind her and stood so close that Jacqui felt the entire length of his body behind her back. He positioned both hands on each side of her waist to steady her. Then his thighs aligned with the back of both her thighs as his feet pushed her ankles open.

"That's one stance…" he whispered in her ear. "And here's another…" he continued. Jacqui's heart hammered wildly in her chest as she felt his palm cross from her waist to her belly then traveled downwards to the front of her crotch. His fingers brushed her mound before proceeding down the front of her right leg. Then his fingers grasped the inner muscle of her thigh before pulling her whole leg backwards. Jacqui felt his hand directly below her vagina.

Seemingly innocent… yet completely intentional. Jacqui knew it. She knew he was pretending to teach her proper boxing posture and copping a feel. She also knew he was toying with her. A primal emotion flared within her… the desire to be conquered. But simultaneously her rational brain told her he was an asshole with a big ego.

If I raise hell, he'll say I have a malicious mind. And laugh at me. If I don't, he'll enjoy himself immensely thinking I'm helpless to do anything about it, were the thoughts in her mind. Jacqui's decision came swiftly. "Two can play this game," she thought to herself as a wicked grin appeared on her face.

The game of seduction was on. "Ohhh…I get it…this feels good," Jacqui said in a husky voice, suppressing the laughter forming in her throat. She let her ass accidentally grind against the front of Adam's crotch and was instantly rewarded with a surprised gasp. She ground her ass even harder this time adding pressure to the swelling bulge inside Adam's pants.

Then she turned her head sideways towards him, opened her mouth and let her tongue follow the outline of her lips. Adam's eyes followed the path of her tongue as it lubricated the skin of her lips. Take that you asshole… Jacqui's inner goddess proclaimed. "How about my hands, Adam… show me the best way to use them," she said in the breathiest voice she could muster.

She proceeded to grab his hand that was still holding her inner thigh. She led his hand slowly upward, letting him feel the swell of her vagina, her flat stomach, and then brushing it gently against her breast. Her hardened nipples gave her away as they screamed in protest against the barrier that was her bra. Even though it started as a game, Jacqui felt the moisture that was slowly forming in her panties. She was enjoying this immensely. Tit for tat. Unfortunately, her body was starting to feel hot.

She had not been with a man since she arrived at boot camp. The fatigue from her daily rigorous routine sucked away all thoughts of fucking for an orgasm. She was doing very well until Adam came along. Heck, he started this. Jacqui tried to ease her conscience. But the feel of a man's hard body against the whole length of her back was just too much to ignore. Plus, Adam smelled of musk and lemongrass soap. A heady combination, given the proximity of their bodies.

Jacqui slumped softly against him, resting the back of her head against his shoulder. Adam's other arm was quick to snake across her waist and pulled her even closer to him until his erection rested between her butt cheeks. From her breasts, Adam's finger followed the contour of her throat, up her chin, and brushed against her lips. Jacqui opened her lips slightly and sucked on the finger before turning slowly around to face him.

"You play hardball," Adam said, his nose inches away from hers, his breath wafting slowly into her face. He was breathing hard and trying to control it. But

Jacqui saw how totally aroused he was as his nostrils flared with every breath he took. "You started it," Jacqui answered petulantly, her own breath came in short gasps. "Then let's finish it before the old man returns," Adam answered.

The thought of Uncle Max catching them in the act sent both into a provocative frenzy. He would be mad as hell, but at this point neither of them really cared. Adam bent down and used both hands to hoist her legs upwards. Jacqui straddled him upright, surprised at the ease in which he carried her. Adam shuffled to one of the corner posts of the boxing ring. Using the post to support her back, he pulled at the drawstring on his pants. They fell and gathered around his ankles.

Using his fingers, he clawed at the sheer material of Jacqui's shorts and tugged hard. The material tore away, leaving her with just her panties. Even that did not escape the ferocity of his fingers as he gave it a twist until it too tore apart. He positioned his cock and lowered Jacqui, who moaned with pleasure as the head of his engorged cock entered her slowly. Her wet pussy lubricated his entire shaft. He rammed into her slowly, and then increased the speed as he ground his hips to reach her even deeper. Grunting with every thrust Adam made, Jacqui clung to Adam's neck like a person drowning. She had never been taken this way before. And the feel of his hard shaft rubbing against her clit was like wildfire consuming her entire being. A shudder ran through Adam's body as a huge orgasm overcame him. He pulled out of Jacqui and pushed her against the mat of the ring. Jacqui shimmied backward in a frenzy until her foot touched the edge of the mat. She used this to brace herself.

Adam opened her legs wide and lowered himself until his face was just inches away from her cunt. He knew from Jacqui's quivering body that she was seconds away from her own release. Using his tongue he flicked at her clit repeatedly. Bolts of white heat shot through her entire being. Pressure mounted inside her, leaving Jacqui weak with desire and craving for release. "I'm coming, don't stop…" Jacqui managed to say as a giant wave of indescribable gratification consumed her. Jacqui closed her eyes tightly, mouth forming a silent "O" as the first of multiple orgasms consumed her. She bucked wildly as her body sizzled. Unknowingly, Jacqui clamped her thighs shut as the pleasure was released, inadvertently pinning Adam between her legs.

Adam laughed softly as he rested his head against her tummy. He smelled her aroma and realized he liked it. He could stay between her legs forever. Jacqui opened her eyes after seeing stars explode inside her brain. Her eyes adjusted slowly to her surroundings as blood started to flow normally inside her body. Breathing normally one more, Adam said, "Round one goes to you, Jacqui. You have managed to pin me and we haven't even started on full contact sports yet."

"Yup, remember that next time you try and seduce me again," a languid Jacqui replied as she opened up her thighs to release him.

Jacqui picked herself up from off the floor, ignoring Adam's outstretched hand. She was more concerned about her nakedness than his gallantry after seeing her shredded panties on the floor. "What… are you still mad at me?" Adam asked, surprised at the display of irritation on her face.

"Asshole…" Jacqui muttered, as she picked up her panties off the floor and headed for the bench where she left her training suit. She felt totally embarrassed in her half ass-naked glory while Adam had his drawstrings back on. Adam's guffaws followed her inside the room, adding fuel to the irritation she felt. She was confused and needed to gather her composure. Jacqui had never been in love before. Growing up, she realized she had an appetite for sex. It was one of the reasons she wanted to get her own place back home. After her family was murdered, she discovered that it could make her forget the daily nightmares that tormented her.

But she's been free from those dreams ever since she arrived at boot camp. Why did she fall for Adam's advances? And, honestly… she did entice him too. Jacqui had no answers so she did the next best thing and filed Adam under the category 'Proceed with Caution.'

Chapter Three

"Great workout, Sarah…" Jacqui said, reaching out her hand to pull up a petite, red-haired girl, who was trying to catch her breath on the mat. Anyone seeing Sarah for the first time would think the girl was barely out of her teens. The freckles that dotted her face and the flat chest simply enhanced the impression. Jacqui found out the hard way that Sarah was badass and can kick her butt even if she barely reached Jacqui's shoulder.

It was Adam who chose the girl as Jacqui's sparring partner in their workouts. This was the first time Jacqui managed to pin Sarah to the ground. After weeks of teaching Jacqui the basic moves of boxing, they moved on to different types of martial arts. Adam was an exacting mentor but a good one… Jacqui had to give him that. He made her do the different moves over and over again until she got them perfectly. Jacqui learned to do the ax kick, foot stomp, superman punch, flying knee, guillotine and rear naked choke.

But to Jacqui's consternation, Adam had only demonstrated these moves to her. Since that day in the boxing ring when they fucked each other like two dogs in heat, Adam had never tried to touch her again. Initially, Jacqui regarded this as a sign of her victory. But as the days passed, her self-righteousness slowly turned to disappointment... one she tried to mask by excelling in everything he taught her. But Adam simply regarded her as his student now and had chosen Sarah to be Jacqui's sparring partner.

During her second week at boot camp, Uncle Max finally introduced her to the rest of the group. Aside from Sarah and Adam, there was Eli, the stern faced, ex-military man who met her at the airport. He was in charge with the high-powered weapons. He was visibly impressed with the successive bull's eyes Jacqui scored in target shooting. Jacqui shrugged it off as a recessive gene she probably got from her dad. And then there was Johnny 'The Eye' Rodriguez, a whiz kid who interpreted data streaming live inside Uncle Max's office.

The rest of the motley crew was made up of men and women from different backgrounds, all with different reasons for why they ended up as bounty hunters. Jacqui had developed an easy camaraderie with everyone, except for Adam. She was quite unsure about her feelings for him. But Jacqui couldn't deny the frustration she was slowly building inside her mind. Why was he so indifferent to her?

She had seen how he was with the other girls. And with Sarah he was always sweet, often giving her a hug after a particularly heavy workout. Jacqui had to content herself with high fives as a sign of his approval. But there were no hugs. Shit…not even a pat in the back, Jacqui thought after she kicked Sarah's ass tonight. Adam signaled the end of practice.

"See you in the mess hall," Adam said casually, turning towards the door. Sarah followed right after giving Jacqui a pat on the back.

Jacqui entered the cubicle to change, her thoughts about Adam's lack of interest still swirling in her mind. "Maybe I should have been sweeter to him that night, instead of playing it cool." She thought back to that particular heavy encounter they had weeks ago. "Yes, that's what I'll do. I'll show him I can be sweet, let him know that I am interested." Jacqui made up her mind.

She switched off all the lights in the room and, opened the door and walked slowly towards the mess hall. As she turned a corner, she was taken aback as she saw the outline of two people locked in a tight embrace within the shadow of the building. She stepped back not wanting to intrude and heard a voice speak out.

"It's alright Sarah, things will work out…" It was Adam's voice that Jacqui overheard. Jacqui's heart stopped for a moment, anxious that she may have been seen. And then as realization set in, anxiety turned into heavy disappointment and regret. So, Sarah and Adam… Jacqui thought, before stepping silently back and fleeing towards the opposite direction.

She went directly into her room and flung herself on the bed.

Confusion over what she had witnessed overwhelmed her. She just couldn't understand why her heart felt like it had been sliced in two. It's not like he means anything to me. We just fucked each other. End of story… Jacqui consoled herself but she was not really feeling any better about it. Deep in her heart she hoped they could take their relationship onto the next level. But now it seemed that wasn't possible. Adam was with Sarah now.

Unwanted tears formed in her eyes. She was startled by a loud rapping on her door as she hastily wiped the tears away. "Jacqui…dinner is ready; we're all waiting for you at the mess hall…" Jacqui recognized the voice of Uncle Max. "Err…Uncle Max, is it alright if I pass on dinner tonight? I have a really bad headache and just want to rest…" Jacqui replied, trying to hide the tears from her voice.

"Of course… rest then… Jacqui, is everything ok? You sound really strange," Uncle Max reacted from outside her door. "Yes…yes… it's nothing, Uncle Max…just need to rest…"Jacqui countered back at him. "Alright then…Jac, I need to talk to you later after we eat. Do you think you can make it to my office around 2100 hours? It's important," the old man said. "Of course…I'll be there," Jacqui replied.

Jacqui took a long shower hoping to wash away her depression. A calm resolution washed over her as the water splashed her clean. I'll forget all about Adam and just focus on what I need to do. Fuck him. I hope he and Sarah have a great fucking time together, Jacqui thought although it left a bitter taste in her mouth.

An hour later, a composed Jacqui walked into the office of the old man. She was dressed in a white floral blouse over a pair of denim shorts and white sneakers. Jacqui was surprised to see they were not alone. She thought that this meeting was strictly between her and Uncle Max. But Adam sat in a dark corner of the room with arms crossed over his chest. He had a dark look on his face, seemingly irritated over something.

Jacqui had a suspicion she was the reason. They both stopped talking abruptly when she entered the room. "Ahh… Jacqui," Uncle Max greeted her, "glad to see you're feeling better." Jacqui remained silent; her eyes avoided the direction where Adam sat in the shadows. Uncle Max ushered her to the same hardback chair where he conducted her first interview the day she arrived. He positioned himself on the opposite side of the desk facing Jacqui. He inhaled a long breath and said, "I think you're ready for your first assignment."

Jacqui was stunned over this announcement. She had been looking forward to this day. She often wondered how much longer she needed to train before she would be allowed to go out and track someone. She had immersed herself on the laws of bail investigations. She was ready to kick some ass. "Really Uncle Max," Jacqui couldn't hide the elation in her voice. Uncle Max pulled out a brown manila envelope and handed it to her. "This just came in. I pulled everything I could about this guy from our sources. Take a look at it tonight. If you think you're ready, then you can start tracking tomorrow by daylight," Uncle Max said.

Jacqui eagerly grabbed at the folder but the old man held back. Jacqui looked at him with a questioning look. "Do you think you're ready, Jacqui?" Uncle Max asked with a hint of skepticism in his voice. "Because Adam here thinks otherwise." "I'm ready," Jacqui answered with a hint of irritation in her voice. And then just as quickly, she added, "I beat Sarah's ass earlier today."

"Sarah has nothing to do with whether you're ready or not," Adam's voice cut coldly as he stood up from the shadows. Jacqui swallowed hard, regretting her outburst. Of course Adam was right. She managed to make it sound petty. Uncle Max had no idea she caught

Adam and Sarah in a tight embrace earlier in the evening. And Adam didn't know either.

"No…err, what I mean is…uhhm…I train everyday with Sarah, so I know I can protect myself if the time comes," Jacqui added lamely. "That's what I was telling Adam before you came in. This case is pretty cut and dried. Get information about his whereabouts… report to me as soon as you have established that. Is that clear, Jacqui?" Uncle Max asked her. Jacqui nodded her head in agreement.

"Ok… that's it then. Unless… you have anything else to add, Adam?" Uncle Max said looking at the grim face of the man who was slowly capturing Jacqui's untrained heart. "Nothing from me. I think I'll call it a night," Adam replied before storming out of the room.

Jacqui had an irresistible urge to run after him, to offer her hand in friendship. Her pride could withstand the humbling experience of extending an the olive branch. She was ecstatic over this new development and wanted everything to be A-OK in her world. But why did he have to be so difficult? She didn't want to make a scene in front of the old man… didn't want to give him any idea about her feelings for Adam.

So Jacqui bade her Uncle Max goodnight but not before giving him a tight hug. "Thanks Uncle Max," she whispered as the old man hugged her back. Holding her at arm's length, Uncle Max said softly, "I didn't want to say this in front of Adam…but… no theatrics, Jac. Bounty hunting is dangerous, but rewarding. Play it straight. Spot your man, report, and then get out of there. Is that clear?"

Jacqui spent half the night reading through the dossier from the brown manila folder. She memorized the features of the man that accompanied the information about him. The hours ticked by and Jacqui became aware of a floorboard creaking outside her bedroom. Warily, she stood from the bed and opened her bedroom door. The hallway was empty. But a strong instinct nagged at her that it was Adam. The smell of lemongrass wafted in the air. But what would he be doing outside her room? She went to investigate but found no one in the hallway.

Shaking her head in disgust over her own foolishness, Jacqui re-entered her bedroom once more, sat cross-legged on the bed and ran through the papers one more time. When weariness finally overtook her, she stuffed all the papers back into the manila envelope, pulled the light switch and spread her tired body over the bed. Maybe this is what I need. A couple of days away from him will do me good. Put things in the right perspective…forget his intoxicating smell, forget the way his arms felt around me, forget his tongue on my…

Jacqui finally drifted away into a troubled sleep.

Chapter Four

Jacqui spotted the man as soon as he stepped out of the van. He was trailed by a group of five heavily armed men as suggested by the bulges in the back pockets of their pants. The rest entered the cabin as one man remained outside the door. This was the fourth day that Jacqui had been hot on their trail. She was in a small town fifty miles from Utah. She was exhausted. She had very little sleep since leaving the boot camp four days ago.

She almost had her quarry yesterday. But something tipped them off and they left in a hurry before Jacqui could phone in their whereabouts. She got her tip from a gas station attendant who filled up her tank. Showing him a picture of her prey, she pretended to be an ex-girlfriend.

"The bastard refuses to pay support. He fucking gives me a baby and then disappears… I heard from one of his buddies he's here somewhere. Just can't wait to give him spit for all the trouble he gave me," Jacqui moaned. "Yer can try some of them cottages for rent two miles from here. Me wife works there as a cleanin' woman. Says there are some newcomers. But she's kinda scared of 'em. Seems they're up to no good…y'know what I mean?" the attendant said.

Jacqui nodded her head trying to contain the excitement she felt. She traveled in the direction the attendant pointed out and now she spotted the cottages hidden among the trees. It was a decrepit resort patronized mainly by travelling salesmen, truck drivers, and road travelers who wanted a cheap overnight stay.

Jacqui scouted the area before taking up her position behind some thick bushes surrounding a small clearing. The cottages were all within her sight as well as the road leading up to the resort. After almost five hours of endless waiting, Jacqui caught sight of a black van with heavily tinted windows moving at great speed. It came to a full stop at a cottage farthest from the road.

Jacqui positioned the binoculars and peered through the looking glass. Her quarry was the last to step out of the van. There was no denying he was the very same man in the photograph in Jacqui's hand. Knowing that every second counted, Jacqui pressed the call button on the cell phone that she carried in her pocket.

The call was picked up on the first ring. "I've got them. It's a small resort two miles from a gas station in a small town called Burkesville, fifty miles outside Utah," Jacqui reported. "I got the location, Jacqui," she recognized the voice of Johnny 'The Eyes' Rodriguez.

Then a familiar voice came onto the line, "Do you have a positive ID?" "Yes Uncle Max, it's him," Jacqui answered. "You got 10 minutes to get the hell out of there before all hell breaks loose…" Uncle Max declared, before cutting the line.

Jacqui stealthily crossed the bushes, crouching low over the trees before hitting the road. Then she ran swiftly toward her car that was parked in a steep embankment a few meters away. She gunned her engine before making a U-turn away from the resort. In the distance she heard the chop-chopping of a helicopter and met a coterie of police cars with flashing red, white, and blue lights headed towards the direction of the resort.

Jacqui knew she had caught her prey. Her first assignment was a success. A feeling of accomplishment and purpose engulfed her. She wanted to laugh out loud in triumph. She had made her first bounty without endangering herself. She was euphoric and was floating on air. And more than Uncle Max, she had an overwhelming desire to share her success with Adam. He had never left her thoughts throughout the four days that she had been away from him. Who gave a shit if he was with Sarah? She could be friends with him. That was as good a start as any she could think of.

Maybe what he had with Sarah wasn't so serious, Jacqui hoped. She could show him she wasn't a bitch. Yes…they could be friends …for now. These thoughts gave Jacqui the second wind she needed to drive all the way back to boot camp. She didn't make any pit stops… not to eat or relieve herself… driven by some primal call to be with Adam.

She only slowed down when she made a turn on the small dirt road that would lead her through the copse of evergreens to the structures that were hidden beneath the trees. Uncle Max came out to greet her as soon as she stepped of the car. He placed his arms around her shoulder, squeezed tightly, and said, "Well done, Jac.

They're all in custody. You've earned your first bounty reward."

A round of cheers and claps met her as she entered the office. Everyone she knew were drinking champagne from paper cups, celebrating her victory. It was an immensely great feeling. Jacqui's eyes swept the room, searching for that one face that had been in the forefront of her psyche. Maybe he hadn't heard about the news yet. Maybe he was on his way to join them? Maybe this time he could at least give her a hug?

"Where's Adam," she asked Uncle Max over the din of the revelry around her. "Adam? Oh…he left a few days ago with Sarah. Said it was something personal. You know Adam. He's full of mystery," Uncle Max informed her. Jacqui felt her world crash and burn all around her. Adam was gone. And he was with Sarah. She thanked everyone, gave an excuse about being beat, and made a hasty retreat to her room.

There was no denying the hot tears as they fell uninvited from her face. There was no denying the crushing pain that wrapped around her heart like a steel band. And most of all, there was no denying the simple truth… she was in love with Adam.

-To be continued in Book 3-

Book Three – Rapid Pulse Bounty

Chapter One

JACQUI SCHNEIDER gazed at her naked reflection in the mirror and liked what she saw. She had always been curvaceous since her breasts started to form when she was sixteen years old. She got that from her mom. But unlike her mom, whose modest virtues bordered on obsessive, Jacqui loved to flaunt her sexiness even as a teenage girl.

But since hooking up with Uncle Max at *The Agency*, the daily rigors of the exercise routines the old man made her go through every day certainly managed to give her muscles the tone that wasn't there before. Her shoulders seemed broader, giving the illusion of a smaller waistline that curved down to her hips. Her round ass was perky as she gave it a playful smack. Her toned arms and legs gave her body the overall impression of a well-oiled machine. Sweating profusely after a five mile run, her sunburned milky-white skin had a pinkish tinge.

After her first assignment went better than expected, Jacqui gained a certain confidence that she never felt before. The next three captures were just as successful. Everything was going well for her. The changes she saw in her body were merely icing on the cake. Every successful capture meant more money in her pocket. It would never replace the loneliness she felt in being alone without mom, dad, and Danny, but it was a good start. Jacqui mulled over in her mind how to spend some of it. Travel, perhaps? But that decision was a long way off from today.

The thought that she would never have to worry about money in the future gave her a sense of security she lost when her whole family was murdered. The easy fifty thousand dollars that she earned from four bounty works had been deposited in the bank, together with the money her dad left her.

"Not bad…" Jacqui whispered in approval over her finances as well as the reflection staring back at her. Picking up the heap of dirty clothes from the floor and grabbing a robe along the way, Jacqui entered the bathroom of her new apartment. Uncle Max helped her settle into her new digs. He insisted that Jacqui come down to the headquarters every day and keep up with her training. So Jacqui opted for a modest townhouse in a quiet neighborhood five miles away. It was a two bedroom affair, furnished, thus sparing her the tedious task of shopping for her own furniture. The living room and kitchen were roomy enough to keep her comfortable during the times she was home.

The only indulgence she added was a shower stall with overhead rainfall shower, a handheld shower hose and 6 body jets. Plus the whirlpool bathtub that Uncle Max declared was a waste of good money. Jacqui insisted that taking long showers was an indulgence and won the argument. This was where she retreated after grueling days of tracking her prey, oftentimes foregoing the luxury of a plain shower when she was on the road. Jacqui adjusted the knobs of the whirlpool and watched as the water churned gently against the edges of the tub.

She lit a few incense candles and poured lavender bath oil into the water.

She stepped gingerly into the warm water and slithered her whole body against the tub. She closed her eyes and sighed in bliss, basking in the floating sensation, making her feel weightless. She allowed her mind to roam, setting free all thoughts and stresses that accompanied her job. But it was also during times like these that thoughts she had buried deep in the recesses of her psyche often crept out of their screened-off area where she had buried them.

Like Adam…

She hadn't seen or heard from him since that day she made her first successful bounty. The revelry that accompanied her return wasn't enough to cover up the intense disappointment she felt when she was told he left with Sarah. She cried herself to sleep that night, after admitting to herself the true status of her heart. She had fallen in love with him… fallen in love with a man who belonged to someone else.

Often, she cursed the day they met. Cursed the seduction he laid out for her. She blamed herself for trying to defeat him in his own game which ended with them having sex on the boxing ring floor. His intoxicating scent, the smell of his breath, the steely feel of his arms around her waist, the powerful thrusts as he entered her astride on his hips.

Jacqui crossed her arms around herself longing for Adam's lean arms. Then she uncrossed them to caress the skin of her throat, shoulders, and belly. They felt velvety and smooth to the touch. Unwittingly, her hands moved to her breasts as she lay immersed in the warm frothy water. She cupped both and let the thumbs and forefingers of each hand play with her nipples. She felt them harden under her ministrations as twinges of sexual pleasure traveled down her groin.

Jacqui enjoyed the feeling of her fingers as they slowly moved down to her cunt. Using two fingers, she opened the lips of her labia and let her clit pop out. The whirlpool massaged her clit gently. It felt really good. She rubbed her exposed nub and added pressure with her finger. Her back arched as a spike of pleasure signaled her arousal. Jacqui raised herself up from the tub and sat down against the rim. She opened her legs wide as she straddled two sides of the tub. She knew what she wanted, what she needed badly.

She picked up a bottle of lube and applied some on her fingers. Then she positioned her fingers against her vagina and rubbed her clit gently. The heat started to build within her open legs. As the heat mounted inside her, Jacqui added more and more pressure on her clit until it felt on fire. She knew her orgasm was near. She imagined Adam's lips as they flicked repeatedly on her clit when he had her prone on the mat. As the intense heat flaring between her legs became too much to bear, she gave in to a powerful orgasm, uttering Adam's name over and over again.

An hour and fifteen minutes later, Jacqui entered the gate of *The Agency* complex. She wanted to practice on the punching bags. Jerking off today left her feeling lethargic. Instead of diminishing the longing for Adam which she had buried deep inside, it left her with the feeling of wanting more.

"A few rounds on the mat may do me some good," Jacqui thought to herself. She dressed up in black compression short shorts which only served to draw attention to her booty. A white razor back t-shirt that ended just above her navel completed her training outfit. Uncle Max saw her arrive in her car and called out to her.

"I have something for you…come inside, Jac," Uncle Max said leaving the door open. He handed her a parcel wrapped in brown paper and tied with a twine. Jacqui eagerly tore open the package and squealed in joy. Inside was a pink and gray Walter PPK handgun. It was slim and at 6 inches long, fitted perfectly in the palm of her hand.

"Oh, Uncle Max, thank you…it's…it's perfect," Jacqui declared as she gave the old man a hug. "Eli and I were discussing the best weapon for you and we both agreed this is it," Uncle Max said, obviously happy they made the right choice for her.

And then as an afterthought, the old man declared, "You're a good shot Jac, just like your dad. Keep up your practice with Eli. Learn the characteristics of your gun until it becomes an extension of your hand." "Yes… yes… I will…" an elated Jacqui replied before dropping the gun into her purse. "Ready to kick some ass?" Uncle Max asked, eying her tight shorts and even tighter tees. "Nah…just the punch bags for now…" Jacqui replied with a wink. "Well…I'm glad coz I don't think anyone will win against you in that outfit…" Uncle Max retorted with laughter in his voice.

The gym was quiet. Nobody was around today using the ring or flexing muscles on the punch bag. This suited Jacqui just fine. She was in no mood for company. She started with five hundred jump ropes to break out a sweat before donning the gloves and approaching the bag hanging from the ceiling. With light punches, she danced around the bag to improve her footwork. Then she moved on to combination punches. She focused her concentration on her fists just like Adam taught her.

"It's not about strength, but how you use your fists to deploy the power of your punch… " she remembered him saying. With every punch the hapless bag took, Jacqui felt she was pounding her unrequited feelings back into the compartment inside her heart where she had reserved a special lock and key for it. She only slowed down when the darkened hall was suddenly illuminated by sunbeams streaming from the doorway as someone entered the room.

Curious to see who the newcomer was, Jacqui stopped momentarily to greet the new arrival. The sun was shining directly into the open doorway. The silhouette was shrouded in the glow coming from the sun overhead. It took Jacqui's eyes a few seconds to adjust from the darkened interiors as she eyed the shimmering form bathed in sunshine. When the newcomer closed the door behind, Jacqui gave a gasp of surprise.

The figure was shirtless, as usual. The denim jeans hung carelessly below the hips, emphasizing the flat stomach and the six pack abs. The hair hanging just above the shoulders still needed a haircut. It had a reddish tint over the burnished brown color that it used to be. The smile still held the same combination of a mock and a naughty grin.

The figure was unmistakable. It was Adam.

Chapter Two

Jacqui was in a state of shock. She didn't know if the figure leisurely walking toward her was a figment of her imagination… a deception her mind was playing on her pining heart.

"Hello Jacqui," Adam greeted her with a nonchalant smile on his face. "Hi…Adam," Jacqui squeaked, her throat barely able to make the words come out. And then she realized she needed to say something more than just a mundane hi.

"Err… you're here… it's nice to see you back… when did you get ba… ?" she managed to stammer words that fell over each other. Fuck, nice didn't even come close. She was ecstatic, euphoric, overjoyed. Now if she could only unfreeze her brain so she didn't sound catatonic. Jacqui reached out her hand to shake his in greeting just as Adam moved forward and clasped her in an embrace.

Another awkward moment… welcome, but totally unexpected. Jacqui hoped he wouldn't notice how wildly her heart was fluttering inside her chest as her feelings struggled to surface from their stronghold.

"Last night…" Adam answered before releasing her from his arms. "Last night?" Jacqui mimicked, feeling like a parrot. "Oh… you arrived last night." "Yah…

Uncle Max has been updating me with things around here. Heard you're doing great," Adam replied with a sideways glance, uncertainty written on his face. What was wrong with her?

"Well, yah… err… thanks…" Jacqui once again stumbled through her vocabulary which seemed to have shrunk to four- or five-letter words. Why did he have such an effect on her composure? Surely he had no idea about her feelings for him. "Uncle Max said I'd find you here… you look great, Jacqui," Adam said eyeing her and obviously liking what he saw.

Jacqui flushed under his intense gaze and felt naked once again. "Feel like doing a round with me?" Adam teased her. "No… no, thanks, I was just cooling down when you came," Jacqui replied although she felt a stab of disappointment. What she really wanted to say was, Hell yeah… bring it on…

Adam laughed at her discomfiture, reading her thoughts. He took a seat in the exact spot on the boxing ring where he fucked her. Jacqui knew that he did it on purpose. As if to remind her of what took place on that mat. "So…fill me in… what happened when you were out there…?" Adam tapped the empty space beside him, inviting her to sit.

Gingerly, as if walking on eggshells, Jacqui positioned herself beside him. She thought she wouldn't have the words to convey to him everything she felt when she was out there all alone. But Adam's encouraging demeanor made it easy. She told him about the long hours of sitting and waiting for her prey to make their appearance, the dismay she felt when she lost track of their whereabouts, the sudden adrenaline rush when she recovered their tracks, her anxiety when she had them within her sight just before she made a call to confirm their location, and the euphoria that accompanied her after each successful bounty.

"Oh, Adam, it's the best feeling in the world…" she gushed. "Better than an orgasm?" Adam asked impishly. Jacqui nudged him playfully with her shoulder. She can be cool with him. After all, she did decide to start a friendship with the rascal. "Oh… I almost forgot… Uncle Max wants to see you in his office," Adam said, jumping from the edge of the boxing ring, holding out his hand to help her down.

Jacqui reached out to accept his assistance, a thrilling buzz running through her palm, up her elbow, through her shoulders and straight into her heart with the sudden contact. She was alarmingly aware that he didn't let go of his grip as they made their way towards the door and out into the open to see the old man.

Uncle Max was sitting behind his table, a stack of documents spread out before him. "Ahh…good…you're both here," he greeted them, indicating the two chairs in front for them to sit on. "Meet Malcolm Leech, 33 years old, originally from Havana, but managed to acquire U.S. citizenship, second in command to an arms dealer who is so elusive, the DEA thinks it's almost impossible to catch him. Leech has a bounty on his head for $750,000 and his boss at a million dollars, caught alive. They supply ammo for the different street gangs - Hispanics, Latinos, Mexicans, and Blacks. Mostly from the Chicago area. No discrimination. You show money, they deliver," the old man informed them.

"Why has the DEA been unsuccessful if they sell to anyone…?" Adam asked. "They have powerful connections… their reach is so high they seem to be always a step ahead of the DEA, who suspects a mole in their department. The DEA realized they couldn't do anything using their own agents so they deployed someone else months ago to do the sting. Word on the street now is Leech has just received fresh delivery, more than they can handle. His boss does not feel it is in safe hands. With too much ammo lying around, it's bound to attract the attention of the authorities. He is pressuring Leech to find buyers, pronto. That's all we know."

"So the DEA approached you, asking help in tracking the whereabouts of this Leech…" Jacqui concluded. But Uncle Max cut in before she could finish her sentence and said, "Not just track the guy, but pose as interested buyers, and hopefully, set up a meeting with the brains behind the organization."

"Do we have a photo of him?" Jacqui asked, curious to see the face of the man behind it all. "Unfortunately, this is all we have," Uncle Max said, handing them a 4x6 glossy. Adam and Jacqui peered at the photograph. It was a grainy shot taken with a telephoto lens from a distance. The man wore a grey overcoat with a hat pulled low over his head. The shot showed part of his forehead, a nose, and a sharp chin, as he was about to board a plane. For some inexplicable reason, Jacqui felt agitated. It could have been a picture of anyone. But the outline of the man was strangely familiar. She shrugged it off, thinking it was just her imagination playing tricks on her.

"That photo was taken less than six months ago and the DEA has no idea where he is hiding," Uncle Max said. Adam and Jacqui handed the pictures back to the old man. He was suddenly very serious. "I want both of you to go in and pose as buyers. As I mentioned, the DEA is afraid there is a mole buried deep within their department. Both of you fit the profile of someone this Leech could trust," Uncle Max pointed out to Adam and Jacqui.

Adam and Jacqui looked at each other. There was a glint of excitement in Adam's eyes. Jacqui was excited about this development. Uncle Max must believe in her, enough to trust her with an assignment this big. That, and the fact that she will be working with Adam made the whole experience seem surreal. She forgot the initial foreboding she felt when she saw the grainy picture of the man behind the organization.

The very next day, both boarded a domestic flight to Chicago. The two-hour and thirty-minute flight was spent going through the minute details of their M.O. and surfing through the internet with a notebook.

Johnny 'The Eye' Rodriguez's expertise with equipment and technology had allowed him to hack through the internet and bombard it with articles about their 'escapades'. There were pictures of both Adam and Jacqui skiing on the slopes of Aspen, running with the bulls in Spain, Adam racing at The Formula One, Jacqui sunbathing in Hawaii, all very realistic, and every single one a complete hoax.

Jacqui giggled at a copy of her photo-shopped bikini clad body, dancing with a glass of wine in her hand. Jacqui had two left feet and never danced in her entire life. "That looks so much like you," whispered Jacqui, pointing to a photo of Adam wearing a black racer jacket and preppy Persols. "That's because it's really me… " he whispered back with a hint of laughter in his voice.

"You used to race?" Jacqui inquired, with amazement in her voice. "Uh-huh… still do…"Adam replied with a nod of his head. "Gosh… there's so much I don't know about you…" Jacqui replied, suddenly feeling aghast about her curiosity.

"What do you wanna know…?" Adam asked casually. "Well for starters, where's Sarah, your girlfriend? I haven't seen her since you got back," Jacqui asked quickly before she could change her mind. Adam let loose a guffaw which attracted the attention of some passengers nearby. Then he stood up and pretended to point at her while drawing circles beside his brain, miming she was crazy.

"Sit down," an embarrassed Jacqui hissed. "For starters, Ms. Busybody…Sarah is not my girlfriend, she's my stepsister. Whoever told you she was, should have their head examined," Adam stated, with a puzzled look on his face.

"Well… err… no one said, really. I just assumed when I caught you two together, locked in an embrace outside the building," Jacqui explained, a wild blush turning her face red. "You were snooping on us?" Adam teased her mercilessly. "No… no… of course not. It was an accident. I didn't know you guys were there until I almost ran into you," Jacqui denied vehemently.

Adam leaned back in his seat and said, "My sister has some serious issues. That night you saw us… she came to me and told me she was above her head in gambling debts with some syndicate. It was her boyfriend who got her hooked. I tracked those bastards down, paid off her debts, but not before breaking some bones. I warned them and her boyfriend that if they ever come near her again, I would kill them. Sarah is now in a facility where I hope she gets her head back on straight."

Jacqui was speechless. She was totally embarrassed by her wrong assumption. But at the same time, her heart was soaring and her brain wanted to explode. Sarah was his stepsister… not his girlfriend. Best news ever. "Wait a minute…is that why you have been acting so aloof, so cold to me…because you thought I had a girlfriend? You were jealous," Adam said with certainty.

Jacqui leaned back with a Mona Lisa smile on her face and closed her eyes, pretending to sleep. In a girl's psyche, when cornered with the truth, the best defense is silence.

Chapter Three

When the plane touched down in Chicago, a limo waiting for them by the curb brought them straight to The Trump Hotel along Michigan Avenue. They were shown adjoining suites that overlooked the Chicago River. It took Jacqui's breath away. Uncle Max pulled out all the stops to create the suitable scenario. After all, two rich kids wouldn't check into a dump.

They had no idea how long it would be before they would hear from the undercover agent who was facilitating the meeting with Leech. This was like a grand vacation for Jacqui, although she didn't want to lose sight of the dangers surrounding the sting. Jacqui ran to her side of the double doors of the adjoining suite and opened Adam's door without even bothering to knock.

A naked Adam greeted her eyes. Obviously, the guy wanted to take a quick shower because he had a towel in his hand. All his discarded clothes were in a pile on the floor. "Oh… oh… oh… I'm so sorry… I should have knocked first…" Jacqui said, her face in flames.

She flew back to her side of the room and shut the door quickly, after which she sagged weakly onto the floor. She could swear she heard Adam's laughter from behind the closed door. "Stupid… stupid… stupid…" she castigated herself, slapping her forehead with her palm.

Picking up the remnants of her lost dignity, she decided she might as well take a shower too. She was feeling sticky after the long flight. Chicago was muggy this time of year.

Jacqui whistled in awe as she opened the door leading to the bathroom. The bathroom occupied half the size of the entire suite. A walk-in closet was on one side with floor to ceiling cabinets in rosewood. The center of the room was occupied by a Jacuzzi with pink marble tiles wrapped around it. The floor tiles, also of pink marble, led all the way to the shower stall in the corner enclosed in Plexiglas. A Tallboy unit held the washbasin just beside the bathroom stall. Gold and crystal accents dominated the room and reflected the lights coming from lamps mounted on the walls.

Jacqui eagerly stripped off all her clothes, forgetting her faux pas with Adam. She entered the stall and lifted her face up the rainfall shower head. The water, which was just the right temperature, felt heavenly as it dripped down her body. The splash coming down from the shower muffled the sound of the shower stall door as it opened. Jacqui hardly noticed that Adam had entered until he whispered in her ear.

"Hope you don't mind if I join you…" Adam said. A startled Jacqui swiveled around. She had no words. Adam lifted her chin up with his finger, their faces inches away from one another. And just before his lips descended down on hers, Jacqui realized it would be futile to resist him. This is what she had been pining the entire time while he was away.

Adam's kiss was deep and probing. He bit gently on her lower lip as his tongue tried to pry them open. Jacqui responded and allowed him access, opening her lips as her tongue met his. Adam reached out behind her to close the shower. His arms then snaked across her back, hands gently exploring the curves leading to her ass. Jacqui was intensely aware of his erection hitting the love spot of her vagina. She reached out her hands to stroke the smooth, hard penis.

Adam grabbed her stroking hand and entwined both arms across his neck before lifting her and carrying her out the bathroom and into the bedroom. He laid her gently across the bed as Jacqui's wet body left an imprint on the satin duvet. Adam stared deeply into her eyes, his prone body atop hers. "Do you want to do this?" he asked her. Jacqui peeled away all reticence and reserve, and answered, "Yes…"

A triumphant smile lit up Adam's eyes before he kissed her again. The kiss was everything Jacqui ever dreamt of. Passionate and romantic, deep and searing, it touched the very recesses of her soul. It was a kiss coming from a soul that was her perfect match… her soul mate.

Adam was a torrid lover. He brought her to heights of passion she did not know existed. He was alternately gentle and savage as he thrust deep into her. Then he would arouse her all over again as he nipped, sucked, and bit her skin. His tongue did not hold restraint as he explored every fold of her pussy, torturing her clit with his unrelenting tongue.

Jacqui thought she had no more to give as her body racked in multiple orgasms. But Adam found reserves

that she did not know she had. When she came again for
the third time, she felt her body would dissolve from the
pleasure. An exhausted Jacqui lay quietly in the nook of
Adam's arm. She had never been more thoroughly
fucked in all her life. She suddenly felt shy being with
him and buried her face into his chest. Adam's arms
were like steel bands holding her tightly next to him.
His next words established what her heart already knew
since the first time they met. "I think I'm in love with
you, Jacqui Schneider," Adam said.

Chapter Four

The call from the undercover agent came at 0600 hours the following day. Jacqui was alerted when Adam pulled away from her as he answered the phone. A few seconds later he turned towards her, still nestled within the covers of the bed and whispered in her ear.

"Sorry babe, it's time," Adam said. Months of training had adjusted Jacqui's mind and body to react swiftly. She half-opened her eyes to see his beautiful face inches away from her own. "Hi…" Jacqui whispered dreamily. How can a face rouse desire within her when half of her was still in slumber? Adam gave a naughty grin, reading her thoughts. He stood abruptly and sighed deeply, regretting the lost opportunity to be inside her once again. He headed straight for the bathroom door. Both knew they had a job to do.

Reluctantly, Jacqui hauled her body up, grabbing the duvet to cover her nakedness. She strode to her own bathroom in the adjoining suite. She wanted to take a long shower and if she joined Adam, who knows where things would lead. No. She had to get her head straight. There was danger for both of them up ahead. It was necessary to have a clear head.

She fought the elation that was bubbling in her chest. Adam was in love with her. He said it. Or did she dream it all? Then she must have dreamt about the way he kissed her, and tenderly suckled her breasts, and made love to her over and over again…

"Stop it, Jacqui Schneider…" she objected to her thoughts. A cold shower was exactly what restored her as she dressed quickly. Adam called through the open doorway that he would be meeting her in the lobby in ten minutes.

As she entered the lobby, she espied him over at the reception counter with a suitcase by his side. "Ready?" Adam asked. Jacqui nodded her head in agreement. She sensed that he was tense, probably more aware than she was about the danger that lies ahead. Carrying the suitcase, he led her to a Mercedes Benz SUV parked in the curb of the hotel. He opened the door and strapped her in.

As he took the driver's seat, he looked at her seriously and said, "Just follow my lead, Jac. I'll do all the talking." "What's in the suitcase?" she asked curiously. "Twenty-five million dollars and this car are all courtesy of *The Agency*," Adam answered simply. Adam punched in an address in the GPS system of the car. They drove through the main thoroughfares of Chicago until they reached the Tri-State Tollway, then onto an inn with a park across the road.

"Leave your gun in the compartment," Adam ordered Jacqui. "But…" Jacqui started to argue until she saw Adam's face. Gone was the Adam who held her all through the night. His eyes acquired a shade of blue like the waters of the ocean in its deepest places. His pupils dilated as he scanned his surroundings. The planes of his face resembled cast metal. A predator, focused, unfeeling, aware of the danger lurking ahead. This was a man who lived for the hunt.

"They will frisk us…" Adam said in a cold voice. Bypassing the reception area, Adam and Jacqui took the stairs to the second floor and knocked on a door at the end of the hallway. The door was opened by a mean-looking Hispanic who eyed them suspiciously. "Leech is expecting us…" Adam said in a steely voice.

The door opened wide as Adam and Jacqui entered a small conference room. The curtains were drawn against the windows. An air-conditioning unit was on full blast while a ceiling fan whirred from above, giving the room its only ventilation.

Malcolm Leech was seated by a table. Prominent among his features were the droopy eyes that stared in a sinister way and a cut on the lip giving him a permanent sneer. A diamond stud gleamed from his ear. Two other men stood on each side. One of them played with a gun in his hand. Adam and Jacqui step into the room and headed for the table. A hand dropped on Adam's shoulder and roughly spun him around.

"Not so fast, Amigo…I need to see you're clean," said man who opened the door. Adam stared him directly in the eyes, indicating his displeasure. After a few seconds, he spread out his arms and legs to allow the search. The man nodded towards the direction of the table to indicate Adam was clean. He reached out to do the same to Jacqui when Adam swiftly grabbed hold of his arm, twisted around and held the man in a headlock. The man squealed in pain.

"You can do a body search on me. But touch my girl and we're both out of here, comprende?" Adam said loudly, looking directly at Leech seated on the table. Leech nodded imperceptibly and Adam let go, pushing the man away from him. Adam picked up the suitcase and ushered Jacqui towards the table. "Leech…" he greeted the man in a sneering voice. "Friend, you have the pleasure of knowing who I am but I know almost nothing about you," Leech said amiably.

"You know enough about me. Otherwise you wouldn't have agreed to meet with us. This is not a social call. I am here for business. Tell me what you've got. I want it all," Adam said in an autocratic voice. Jacqui saw Leech blanch in surprise as Adam's words caught him totally by surprise. "We have single shot rifles, an odd assortment of handguns, AK-47s up to military grade assault rifles," Leech reeled off the entire arsenal in their possession.

"That's fine with me…" Adam answered without batting an eyelash. "Can you make the delivery within two days?" Leech hesitated for the first time… a reaction that didn't go unnoticed by both Adam and Jacqui. "Wait… wait a minute…" Leech faltered. "I need to talk to my partner about this."

"I was told you are the man to talk to. Not some fucking runner for someone else," Adam replied with a note of mockery in his voice. Leech showed his displeasure over the insult and stood up menacingly. But Adam was quick to push his advantage. "Look Leech, I came here prepared to pay…" as he opened the suitcase and displayed the bundles of money within,

"…not negotiate. You bring your partner here now, or else we walk," Adam upped the ante.

"That's impossible. He never meets with anyone. I do all the negotiating," Leech blustered as he eyes the layers of cash within the suitcase. "Then this is all a waste of my time," Adam said with irritation. He snapped the suitcase shut and walked to the door with Jacqui quickly behind him. Both were aware this was the biggest bait they could play. Either Leech takes the bait or they leave empty-handed.

"Hold on…" Leech called out just as they reached the door. Adam turned around to face him, and raised his brows in an arrogant manner. Leech pulled out his cell phone and talked in a low voice. It was obvious from his face that whoever was at the other end of the line was not happy about the turn of events. Leech gesticulated wildly with his arms, trying to make a point. Then he listened intently, nodded his head, smiled and snapped the phone shut.

"He will be here in twenty minutes. You owe me, man…I convinced him you're worth it…" Leech bragged. Adam felt Jacqui's sigh of relief. But he admired her composure. Her face never lost the insipid but haughty look she wore since the start. Both approached the table once more. Now that the tension had broken between them, Jacqui noted that Leech was friendlier… salivating over the money he would earn.

Jacqui knew she needed to make her move. Fanning her hands to her face, she addressed Adam, "Honey, this room is too warm. I need a breath of fresh air…" The man who met them at the door instantly tensed and made as if to follow her as she headed for the door.

Adam spoke with a pleasant voice and tapped Leech by the shoulder. "Tell your man to leave my girl alone. I don't trust him. I mean, after all, what can a little lady do except roll in bed with you?" Leech and the rest of men, together with Adam, chuckled over this. Jacqui pretended to be displeased and left the room with a snooty swing of her hair. As soon as she hit the hallway, Jacqui hurried down the stairs and headed straight for the SUV. She retrieved her Walter PPK and strapped it between her thighs. She left her purse lying on the table inside the room with Adam. Her cell phone was inside the purse. She would need that later on to make contact. But not yet… the primary target had still to show up.

Jacqui's heart accelerated with excitement. If all goes well today, she would be earning lots of money from this bounty. She could afford to take a vacation, hopefully with Adam along. They could do Hawaii. Her picture was all over the internet anyway, dancing with a glass of wine in her hand. Jacqui glanced at her watch. Twenty minutes were almost up.

God, I hope they don't frisk me when I come in again, she thought nervously. The gun between her thighs was the only protection she and Adam had. But she need not have worried, as everyone hardly looked up when she entered the room once more. They were all huddled around Adam, who was showing them some high powered gadgets on his tablet.

Jacqui knew that Adam intentionally did this to divert attention. He was establishing a bond with all the men, making them feel he was one of them. Nice move, Jacqui thought.

The door opened and everyone looked up. Standing on the threshold was a man of about 60 years of age. Silver streaks of hair were showing beside the temple over a hat that covered the rest of his head. He had a hooked nose, and a pointed chin. Except for the eyes that glinted, one would think he was somebody's grandfather. Jacqui sensed the evil lurking behind those eyes. Leech and the rest of his men all stand respectfully as the commandant approached. It was apparent from their demeanor that this was someone they all feared. The imperious leader cast Jacqui a glance as he passed, and proceeded to approach Adam, who didn't bother to stand.

That one glance was all it took. Recognition was instant as memories come flooding back to Jacqui. This… this was the man she saw that night her family was murdered. This was the man who mercilessly shot her mom before her dad's eyes. This was the man who brutally wiped out the light from Danny's eyes as her dad screamed in rage and fear... the man who ended her dad's life without hesitation.

Jacqui recoiled in a mixture of rage and fear. Her breath came in short gasps as the whole room turned red before her eyes. It took immense effort to stop her body from shaking. She had a clear sight of the back of the old man's head. She could draw the gun from between her thighs and pull the trigger. She knew she could kill him with a single bullet. That would be her revenge for the death of her entire family.

Yet somehow, as all these thoughts swirled in her mind, Jacqui knew his death by her hand would only avenge her. What of all the other crimes this guy had committed to others? This man had to be caught and made to suffer for all the evil he had done. Besides, she was the only one with a gun. Adam was unarmed. Jacqui was certain that with the first gunshot, Leech and all the others would draw their own weapons and start shooting. How many could she take down before Adam got shot? She had to think about Adam too.

Jacqui made a quick decision. She played the beautiful, but asinine girlfriend in this scenario. So she sauntered toward the table, grabbed hold of her purse and declared petulantly, "This is taking longer than I thought. I have to cancel a previous appointment."

Adam waved her off as if humoring a child and continued to huddle with the rest of the group. He was playing his role to perfection. Jacqui casually got her phone from her purse and pressed a number. The alarm was sent instantly. The GPS system in the car was wired to show their location. All Jacqui and Adam had to do was wait.

Less than five minutes after sending the call, all hell broke loose as the door was smashed open. Breaking glass flew everywhere as men entered through the windows. The room was a chaotic scene as the S.W.A.T. team in full military gear flooded into the room. Red dots from sniper sights spotted the heads of the old leader, Leech, and the three others. It would have been foolish for them to even try and aim their guns as it would mean instant death. They knew it. The leader knew it.

"It's over..." he muttered under his breath, raising his hands in surrender. Suddenly, a familiar figure entered the room and headed straight for Jacqui. "Uncle Max," Jacqui said in surprise. "You're here. It's him,

Uncle Max. That's the man who killed my whole family."

Jacqui hated to show any sign of weakness, not with Adam and Uncle Max there. But the extent of her emotions got the better of her and she started to cry. Uncle Max hugged her and softly said, "Yes, I know Jacqui. I couldn't tell you earlier because I was afraid your sentiment would get you. I didn't want you to be reckless and make stupid mistakes in your desire for revenge. I know you well enough to know that as soon as you made the connection, you would do the right thing."

"I made a drastic mistake. I should have made sure I killed everyone in your family that night. Then this could have been avoided," the leader declared so casually, as if they were making small talk around the dinner table. Jacqui stared in shock, unable to believe what she just heard. After everything, he still had the gall to taunt her. All the anger she had managed to control till then came flooding back. Anger turned to rage, and rage into boiling fury. She moved away from Uncle Max and ran toward the leader.

"No… no… Jacqui don't," she heard Adam and Uncle Max shout in unison. But Jacqui was beyond control. The potency of her fury gave her feet wings, dashing towards the leader. She raised her elbow, pulled back her arm, closed her fist, and lunged at the leader with a solid punch in the face. The leader fell to a heap on the floor, senseless. Adam could barely restrain a livid Jacqui, even with his arms wrapped around her.

"My girlfriend is pretty cool. She can kick ass," Adam said for all to hear.

<<◇>>

Eighteen months later, a verdict of 'guilty for multiple counts of illicit arms dealing and multiple murder charges' was handed down by the Supreme Court. Jacqui made it her personal mission to attend all the trials. It was with huge relief when she heard the verdict and the sentencing – life imprisonment with no possibility of parole – for the whole syndicate. The rest of the gang, who eluded arrest, vanished into thin air. There was no chance of regaining ground with the arrest of both Leech and the leader of the group.

A day after the sentencing, Jacqui walked slowly to the graves of her mom, dad and Danny. It was a cool day with a gentle breeze. Jacqui laid down the flowers she held in her arms. "I got him, dad. I got him for you, mom and Danny…" she whispered as lonely tears form in her eyes.

A second figure joined her as she stood vigil beside the graves. Adam snaked his arm across her waist and gave her a kiss on the cheek. "Say your final goodbyes, Jacqui. There's a whole new life ahead of you…and if you will allow me, I want to be a part of it," Adam said. Jacqui looked up at him and saw the light in those beautiful blue eyes. Her spirit felt free for the first time in a long while. "Yes…" she answered softly.

It was time to move on.

-The End-

If you enjoyed this series, I would appreciate your leaving a review of the book. Good reviews encourage an author to write as well as help books to sell. Good reviews can be just a few short sentences describing what you liked about the book without having a spoiler. If you could spend 30 seconds writing a review, I would appreciate it: you can review this title right now at your favorite retailer.

Here is a preview of **another story** you may enjoy:

Fifty Recipes For Disaster: A New Adult Romance Series - Book 1

"**ALL RIGHT**, chefs, you have ninety seconds to get your food plated and presented. If your dish isn't ready, you will automatically be eliminated."

My cooking instructor, Chef Michelle Lee, walks through the room, examining our stations. My fellow cooking students and I are competing for the chance to enter another competition. The winner of today's cooking challenge will get the chance to compete for a full-time apprenticeship at Fission, one of Austin's hottest restaurants.

I'm not confident in many aspects of my life, but I know I dominate in the kitchen. I begin plating my dish just as Chef Lee approaches my station.

"Your food presents beautifully as usual, Kiara," she tells me with a smile. "If it tastes as good as it looks, you've got this in the bag," she adds with a soft whisper.

The instructors at *Le Cordon Bleu College of Culinary Arts* aren't supposed to show favoritism to their students, but Chef Lee keeps a soft spot for me. Along with being one of my teachers, she's also my faculty adviser, and she knows the unusual circumstances that brought me to the school.

"Time's up," she calls out to the class. "Place your finished plates on the head table."

I walk my plate to the front of the room and place it on top of the placard that holds my student ID number.

My classmates follow suit… several of them glare at me after looking at my dish. I am delighted, knowing they're all both jealous and impressed I was able to execute a well-developed *Cioppino* within the given time frame. My rich seafood stew is accompanied by fresh sourdough loaves. I examine my classmates' dishes and feel my chances of winning are good.

"Clear away your stations," Chef Lee directs. "Chef Lawton will be here shortly to judge your plates, and I don't want any evidence of who made what on display when he arrives."

Chef Lawton is the *sous* chef at Fission and the judge of this stage of the apprenticeship competition. I clear my station quickly and then I take a seat at the front of the room. I want to be able to see Chef Lawton's expressions as he tastes each dish.

As I sit nervously in my chair, my classmates finish clearing their stations. I can tell everyone else is just as anxious as I am… we've received plenty of critiques from our instructors but this will be the first time a professional chef from a restaurant will be tasting our food. The door of the classroom opens and a tall man wearing a black chef's jacket enters the room.

"Chef Lawton, it's so lovely to see you," Chef Lee welcomes him. "I can't tell you how excited we are to participate in this competition."

"We're excited as well," Chef Lawton replies. "We're always looking for new, innovative chefs at Fission. I'm looking forward to tasting the dishes and welcoming one of your students into the final leg of the competition. I see that all of the plates are ready. If it's all right with you, I'll get started."

"Of course," Chef Lee agrees.

I try not to hold my breath as I watch Chef Lawton sample each of the plates. I feel encouraged when he reaches mine. Instead of sampling one bite and moving on, he holds the broth in his mouth for a moment, and then tastes each type of seafood in turn. The expression on his face tells me that my stew is perfect, and I say a silent prayer I haven't been out-cooked by any of my classmates.

"First off, I'd like to say this is an impressive display," the seasoned chef begins. "Everything on this table is up to par with the level of skill and talent I expect to see from second-year students. That being said, there is a clear winner. One chef not only executed a delicious dish, but also added a few subtle, original touches that showed innovation and creativity."

Adrenaline rushes through me as he moves to stand behind my dish. "Who created this *Cioppino*?" he asks.

I blush involuntarily as I raise my hand.

"And what is your name, Chef?"

"Kiara Sands," I reply, trying to mask the excitement in my voice.

"Well, Chef Sands, it's an honor to welcome you to the next stage of the competition. I look forward to tasting more of your food as the weeks progress. I am needed back at Fission, but Chef Lee will provide you with the details of your new position." He turns to the rest of the class. "To the rest of you, don't be discouraged. You all provided me with excellent dishes, and you have bright futures ahead of you."

"Thank you, Chef," the class responds in unison.

Chef Lawton makes a quick exit, and Chef Lee takes his place behind the head table. "Excellent work today, class. You're dismissed until tomorrow," she announces. My classmates gather their things and leave the room… I stay behind to talk to Chef Lee.

"Kiara, I'm so proud of you." She beams once we are alone. "As you know, there will be two other chefs competing with you at Fission. You're the only one who's been selected from *Le Cordon Bleu,* and I know you'll represent us well." She moves to her desk and pulls a large package from her bottom drawer. "Here is your apprenticeship packet. You'll receive your Fission jacket when you report for work tomorrow morning. If you have any questions, or just need someone to talk to, you know where to reach me."

"This seems like a wonderful dream, and part of me is afraid that I'll wake up any minute now," I confess.

Chef Lee gives me a maternal smile. "This is a dream, Kiara. It's your dream. And you're well on *your* way to achieving it."

<<◇>>

The information packet Chef Lee presented me with instructs me to be at Fission at 10:00 am. I check my dashboard clock as I pull into the parking lot… 9:40 am. I feel smug, knowing I'm probably the first of the three competitors to arrive. I check my makeup in the rear-view mirror before exiting my car.

Fission is housed in a modern brick building in East Austin, one of the city's burgeoning hipster areas. The area gives off a relaxed, laid-back vibe, but I know the kitchen of Fission will be anything but.

I push open the heavy, solid oak door and am greeted by a pixy-sized hostess with spiked, lavender hair.

"Table for one?" she asks me brightly.

"No," I reply nervously. "My name is Kiara Sands. I'm supposed to start work today."

"Oh! You're one of the newbies!" She says warmly. "I'm Megan. It's a pleasure to meet you. The other two are already here. I'll show you to their table."

Damn it! I'd been so sure I'd make the best impression by arriving first, and here I am, the last of the apprentices to report for our first day.

Megan seems to sense my disappointment. "Don't worry. Paul doesn't give a shit how early people show up. As long as you're here when you're scheduled, you'll be fine. And you haven't missed anything. The other two have just been sitting alone since they got here," she offers reassuringly.

"Thank you for that," I say half-heartedly. As I follow Megan through the restaurant, I'm struck by the eclectic, well-placed décor. All of the tables are made of the same polished oak as the front door. The water goblets on the tabletops are tinted in hues of blue, green, and rose… a selection of art from all around the world adorns the walls. The ambiance is on the right side of the fine line between cozy and overwhelming. The restaurant offers a large main dining room, with smaller, more private rooms on each side.

"This is a beautiful place," I say as Megan leads me toward the back of the main room.

"It is," she agrees. "Paul handled all of the decorating himself. He says that Austin is a melting pot, and he wants all of our customers to feel at home when they dine here."

I'm about to comment on how successfully that goal had been achieved when we arrive at a table occupied by a beautiful blonde woman and a swarthy man with sandy blond hair. A pot of coffee and three cups sit on the table.

"Kiara Sands, this is Jenny Foster and Robbs Martin," Megan introduces us. She checks her watch before speaking again. "It's a quarter to ten, so I imagine that Paul will be out shortly. I suggest you get fully caffeinated and enjoy this time off your feet. It will be the last one for today," she warns with a friendly, knowing tone.

I take a seat in the chair next to Jenny as Megan moves back to the hostess station. "It's a pleasure to meet you both," I offer.

"It's a pleasure to meet you too," Robbs replies. "Congratulations on making it this far in the competition. And I'd like to apologize right now for how thoroughly I'm going to kick both of your asses. This job is mine." He speaks with a blend of arrogance and sarcasm, and I can tell immediately that Robbs and I are not going to get along.

Personal relationships are something I struggle with. In my experience, there's no point in getting close to someone who will inevitably let you down. I prefer to keep my head down and focus on getting my job done. As Chef Lee said yesterday, I have a dream and I'm well on my way to achieving it. I'll be damned if I let Robbs or anyone else get in my way.

"Just ignore Robbs," Jenny advises me. "He thinks that he's God's gift to food... women too, probably." She giggles. "So Kiara, what's your story? Which campus were you plucked from?"

"I'm in my second year at *Le Cordon Bleu*," I answer with pride. In my opinion, *Le Cordon Bleu* is the best culinary school in the area—it's also the hardest to get in to. Jenny seems impressed by my background, but Robbs laughs and dismisses it immediately.

"The *Bleu* is all right, I guess," he snorts, "if you're happy being complacent and doing everything old-school."

"I wasn't aware that being classically trained is a bad thing," I reply shortly. "Tell me, what culinary Mecca do you hail from?"

"*Escoffier*," he answers with a cocky smile. "You know, where all of the innovative, cutting-edge people attend. Three of my instructors were nominated for the James Beard award. So like I said, no hard feelings, but I'm going to kick both of your asses. *Escoffier* specializes in farm-to-table cuisine, so I'm exactly the kind of chef Fission is looking for."

I dismiss his statement with a glare. While the *Auguste Escoffier School of Culinary Arts* is reputed for turning out fantastic chefs, in some culinary circles it's dismissed as a hipster college that prioritizes food trends over basic technique and skill.

I don't feel like debating the merits of my education with Robbs, so I turn to Jenny. "And where do you go?" I ask pleasantly.

"The Art Institute," she replies. "I'm still not positive that cooking is my life's passion. I wanted to go to a college that offers other programs, in case I decided to change my major."

"If you're not sure that you want to be a chef, then what the fuck are you doing here?" Robbs asks hotly. "You should give your spot to someone who knows that this is what they want."

Jenny's green eyes fill with both anger and embarrassment, and I can tell she's fumbling for a response.

"I don't agree with that at all," I say warmly. "What better way to find out if you enjoy working in a real kitchen, than by actually doing it?"

"That's exactly what my instructor said when I won this spot," Jenny says with a nod.

"I see how it's going to be," Robbs interjects with more sarcasm. "The two of you are going to band together in 'sisterhood' and gang up on me."

"That's not how it's going to be at all," a firm voice says from behind me. I turn to see one of the most attractive men I've ever laid my eyes on. He's tall, with broad shoulders, blue eyes, and sandy blond hair. He's also wearing a black chef's jacket, identical to the one Chef Lawton wore when he judged my dish. He holds eye contact with me for several moments before he speaks again.

"This competition will come down to one thing and one thing only... the quality of your food. Only one of you will be named my new apprentice, so ganging up on each other won't serve any purpose. I'm Paul Weston, and I'd like to welcome you to my restaurant." He extends his hand to me.

I respond with a firm handshake and a smile. "I'm Kiara Sands. Thank you for this opportunity."

"You're here because you deserve to be. No thanks are necessary," he assures me.

If you enjoyed this sample then look for **Fifty Recipes For Disaster: A New Adult Romance Series - Book 1**.

Here is a preview of **another story** you may enjoy:

Torrid Exposure - Book 1

"I THINK it looks nice."

"Are you crazy? It isn't even at all."

"Well, you do it then, April."

I sigh and take a step forward, looking at the photo that Emily had hung up in the living room. It looks crooked to me. Okay, maybe just a little off center. I lean forward and nudge it slightly with my finger. It slides just over enough to look perfectly center to me and I look back at her.

Emily is wearing an amused expression on her face. "Oh, yeah, massive difference."

I know she is teasing me. I roll my eyes and look back at the photo. I hear Emily leaving the room to go finish unpacking in her own bedroom. I look around the living room. The big things seemed to be unpacked. I sit down on the couch and sink into it, relaxing my feet for a moment.

Moving felt as if it had taken ages. I am glad to see that the big things are all unpacked. Now I can try to relax for the night. Even though it is hot outside, part of me wants to bundle up underneath a pile of blankets and go to sleep.

But I get up and make myself walk to my own bedroom. *My own bedroom.* It sounds foreign to me. Not that I haven't ever *had* my own bedroom. Of course, I had my own bedroom when I lived at home. But I shared a dorm room in college so I wasn't exactly dealing with the utmost of privacy.

Now, however, I have a space all to myself. The only other person in this apartment is Emily, my best friend since I was little. Finally, it feels as if life is falling into place.

I sit down on the floor and start going through one of the boxes. I have always been terrible at packing. I usually end up shoving everything in boxes without any sort of organization at all. I never learn, apparently, because this current box has everything from clothes to my laptop. At the bottom, I yank something out. It is a photo album. This is weird… I didn't put this in here.

I flip it open to a random photo and see myself at age six. My skinny arms are wrapped around my sister, who is beaming at the camera. Behind her is a water slide. We must have been at some water park.

I scowl. My sister, Spencer, must have slipped this in the box. It was most likely a last ditch attempt at getting me to reach out to her.

"It isn't going to work," I say out loud and shove the photo album back in the box.

Emily sticks her head in inquiring, "Did you say something?"

"Yeah. Not to you though. Just…" I bite my bottom lip, "… just that Spencer shoved this stupid photo album in one of the boxes. I didn't notice it until now."

Emily is staring at me, clearly trying to figure out what to say next. She, of all people, knows the relationship I have with my family and that it isn't the best. But I don't want to ruin our day of getting our own place with mention of them so I quickly shake my head.

"No, it's cool, really. I'm just going to finish unpacking in here."

"Okay," she replies and turns around to leave before hesitating. "Listen, April. You know if you need to talk about them, you can. You don't have to lock it all up inside."

"I know. Thanks."

Emily nods at me and leaves me alone in my bedroom again. My earlier zest at having my own space is now slightly dulled. I sit on the floor and run my fingers over the cover of the photo album. I don't know when Spencer would have snuck this in. Did she really think this would do anything? Knowing her, she probably thought I would see it and decide to move back home.

Well, she is wrong. I stand up and decide to go through another box. If I find another surprise from her in any of these boxes, I am going to lose it on her. But I then think quickly, maybe that is what she wants me to do.

I decide I'll unpack something I like. The big box holding my photography equipment is stacked up against the wall. I yank it over and sit down on the floor again, opening it up and slowly pulling everything out.

Once I am holding my camera, I feel myself calm down a bit. It is state of the art. All my equipment is expensive – and I had purchased it all by myself. No hand-outs from Mommy and Daddy, no matter what anyone may think. I go through the box and organize everything. I was itching to take photos of my room and I took some spontaneous shots. I want to start a photo album of my life beginning with moving out on my own and continue on as I get my career going.

After I finish taking some photos of my room, I grab clean clothes and head into the bathroom for a quick shower. I can hear Emily talking to someone quietly on her phone in the kitchen. It is probably her boyfriend. Ever since Matt and I broke up, she is worried that if I hear her talking to her boyfriend, I might start crying over my failed relationship.

Maybe I would have a couple of months ago. But I am working every day to get over Matt and everything we went through. I tell myself that what we had was just a college romance. Of course it was going to end after graduation. That was what I told everyone after we broke up. I downplayed how serious we were. I felt like a fool for not seeing it before it happened.

Only Emily knew how hard the break-up hit me. Better not to think about Matt now. I have other things that I need to focus on. Whatever I went through with Matt is in the past now.

I step into the shower to clear my mind. I have things to get arranged. No use in thinking about the past.

If you enjoyed this sample then look for **Torrid Exposure - Book 1**.

Here is a preview of **another story** you may enjoy:

Romeo Alpha: A BBW Paranormal Shifter Romance - Book 1 by Darla Dunbar

AMANDA WONDERED how the hell she had gotten so far away from home. When she walked, she usually didn't go past a couple of blocks, but she felt so different today. Something was pushing her further and in a different direction, and she wasn't sure what it was. But she didn't care at the moment, because she just wanted to walk.

Not thinking twice about where she was going, she let her gut instinct give her the direction she needed.

Her grandmother had always told her to go with her gut. She'd said human instinct was better than anything. "Intuition is a girl's best friend," she would say, and then they would both laugh. Talks she and her grandmother had always seemed to pop into her head at the strangest of times, like now.

Here she was, going for a walk, and wondering why she wanted to go in a different direction, and there was her grandmother's voice in her head, propelling her along. Amanda missed her grandmother more with every passing year.

Amanda paused and thought about her life thus far. She had just graduated from college and started working in the local animal hospital, but it wasn't quite like she had thought. She didn't see the care and passion she'd hoped to find in the industry. In the city, being a vet was all about how much money you could make, how many pets you could treat. And, at twenty-four, it was hard to be taken seriously.

Her two female roommates were nice, but they all just went their separate ways. They didn't eat ice cream and watch movies like on *Friends*. They didn't share secrets or even laugh or hang out. They really just slept in the same apartment, and they usually weren't even home at the same time. Except Amanda, that is.

Amanda was always at home, it seemed. She had nowhere else to go, really. The other two girls spent most nights out with their real friends or their boyfriends. Amanda lived a lonely life, but she was happy. At least, she was pretty sure she was happy. After all, she had an upstanding career, and she still had money left over from her savings.

Both her parents had been killed in a car accident years ago. Amanda had graduated from high school with no family there that day or on the day she graduated from college. It was what it was, though, and she knew that her parents watched her from Heaven.

The only positive thing was that her parents had been prepared and had made sure they left enough money and a big enough life insurance policy to help her out. They would be surprised but happy knowing how much that money had helped her in the years after their death. She was proud to say that she was able to live off of it through her college years. She'd never even had to get a job like most kids did. Amanda had been able to focus on her classes.

That freedom wasn't worth it, though. She would have worked three jobs at a time while going to school for one more day with her parents.

However, the account was finally starting to dry up, and she needed to think about what she would do. Sure, she had a new job that could pay her bills, but those loans were piling up with interest. Even a vet job only went so far.

Amanda sighed as she began the trek back toward the house.

Amanda liked her walks in the evening. It helped her to relax, enjoying the quiet time alone. And while Amanda wasn't overweight by any means, it helped slim her waistline, which showed those extra biscuits she liked every now and again.

She turned and began to make her way back to the townhouse she shared with her roommates, but stopped as she heard a noise.

A rustling came from behind her, and she turned to see the bushes shaking. Looking over to the other side of the sidewalk, she saw those bushes shake as well. Not wanting to wait around to find out what was behind the leaves, she took off at a run. She swore she heard a growl come from behind her, but she didn't turn to see what was chasing her. That would only slow her down. As she reached the door to her home, she quickly turned the knob and went through headfirst. Shutting the door quickly, she looked out the window. She got a glimpse of a long black furry tail as something ran around to the side of her building.

"What in the world are you doing, Amanda?" Betsy stood there looking at her inquisitively.

"Something was chasing me."

"What?"

"I don't know what it was, but something big and furry was chasing me. I saw a long black tail just now when I walked into the house."

"You mean when you dove into the house?" Betsy's grin faded. "I'll call the game warden. If there is a big animal outside, then none of us need to go out there until they find it and get rid of it."

"Well, I don't want them to kill it."

"I know, silly, but if it's a wild animal, they can take it out to the National Forest and let it loose. The city is no place for a wild animal." Betsy turned and picked up the phone from the receiver.

Amanda stood in shocked silence as she listened to her roommate tell the person on the other end of the phone what had happened.

She knew from Betsy's tone that she and the person on the other end of the phone were questioning her sanity. They lived in a big city, and the closest thing they got to a wild animal was a stray cat or two. They didn't even get raccoons. If there was some huge animal like she thought, then it would make headline news.

Shaking her head in aggravation, Amanda turned toward her room. She suddenly felt silly and didn't want to have to explain what she saw to any more people.

"Amanda? Where are you going? They are on their way and might need to talk to you."

"Tell them it was a dog. Now that I'm thinking about it, it kind of looked like that couple that lives down the road's greyhound. Maybe he just got out."

"Are you sure, Amanda?" Betsy asked, turning and saying something into the phone.

Without saying another word, Amanda shut the door to her room tight and then quickly locked the door. She looked over her room and, seeing the window open and the curtains blowing in the breeze, she ran over to push the window pane down and lock it tight. As she stood there, she looked out into the woods that made up her backyard. There, in the distance, two yellow eyes stared back at her.

Suddenly, more eyes appeared, and it seemed the animals went on forever. She was amazed, since the woods behind her house were very dense and small. The dark night was lit with a full moon. A shiver raced through her as she stood there and stared into the first set of yellow eyes. She quickly shut the curtains and went to sit on her bed. She didn't think she would ever be able to fall asleep knowing what was out there. As she laid her head on the pillow, her mind wondered to large beasts with yellow eyes and sharp fangs. But she was soon fast asleep.

Amanda awoke with a yawn. It had been almost a month since the incident with what she now called a dog. She had agreed with Betsy that her mind had been playing tricks on her that night. There were often times when she was sure she felt eyes on her, and she would turn in one direction or another, looking. What she was seeking, she didn't know, but somewhere in the back of her mind, she just wanted to know if the eyes she had seen that night had been real or just part of her dreams that evening. She was still so uneasy about it that her walks seemed to get earlier and earlier each evening.

She was just about to walk out the door when her phone started ringing. She quickly grabbed it and pushed the button to answer it.

"Hello."

"Ms. Walker?"

"Yes?"

"Hello, Ms. Walker, my name is Ernest Montgomery. I am calling to tell you that your aunt has passed away."

"My aunt? But I don't have any family. You must have the wrong Ms. Walker."

"No, ma'am. Your father was Joshua Walker, correct? Mother Maureen Walker?"

"Yes."

"Then, I have the right Ms. Walker. It is your father's sister I am referring to. She unexpectedly passed away from a heart attack. I am very sorry for your loss."

"Oh, my gosh! I never knew I even had any family. I am very sad that I didn't get to meet her."

"Yes, ma'am. I'm sure. She was a nice woman. I have also called you to see if you can meet with me. I need to go over her will with you."

"Her will?"

"Yes, ma'am. Your aunt was a wealthy woman."

"Oh? Um, okay. When would you like to meet?"

"The sooner, the better."

"Okay. How about today?"

"That would be great. I am in Slatesville, in the valley."

"Oh. Okay. That is just forty-five minutes from me. I can be there in a couple of hours."

"Sounds good, ma'am. I am at the *Montgomery Law Firm*. I am the only attorney in the town."

"Okay. Thank you, sir. I will see you soon."

"Yes, ma'am. I'll be waiting."

Amanda fell back on the couch, stunned, for what seemed like forever. Everything was pushed to the back of her mind as she thought about what she had just learned. She had a family. Well, she *did* have a family. Now her aunt was gone. Could there be others in her family who she knew nothing about? She didn't know, but she did know one thing. She wasn't going to find out sitting around here, twiddling her thumbs. She needed to get going fast.

Amanda headed for the kitchen. She wasn't surprised to see that no one was there. Of course her roommates weren't home. They were either in class or with their boyfriends.

Smiling, she made a cup of coffee and drank it slowly, thinking about what she might find out. Then, with a deep sigh, she made her way to her car. She looked at the small Honda with pride. It was a pile of junk to some, but it held a special place in her heart. She hadn't been able to get rid of her father's car. Instead, she had sold her own.

She looked down at the small picture he had taped to the dash near the speedometer. She was about six in the picture, and she had been holding her mom's cheeks in her hands as she kissed her.

She remembered the day like it was yesterday. They had just got to a cabin they vacationed in. She had enjoyed herself so much. The little cabin had one bedroom with a queen-sized bed where her parents slept and a set of bunk beds for her. They had stayed up late roasting marshmallows as her father told her scary stories about wolves and vampires. She had ended up in their bed, snuggled between the two of them. They had spent the next day hiking and walking trails and seeing tons of waterfalls and animals.

She had loved it and had never forgotten. It soon became a family tradition to go camping every year. After some of those trips, they didn't return home. Instead, they moved on to a different location. The constant moving had been hard on her as a kid, but she would have never told her parents that. She had felt like they were hiding something from her. Of course, she had been young back then and had blown it off as childhood curiosity. Now, with this new family member, she wasn't so sure.

Her parents had been very quiet people. They seemed cautious of everything going on around them and were even a little jumpy at times. Maybe there was more going on here than she thought. She needed to find out.

She wiped away a tear and go in the car. The car had a huge dent in one side and was almost fifteen years old, but it got her where she needed to go. She slid the car into drive and smiled to herself.

"Dad would be proud that his car was still running so good, wouldn't he, Trixy?" She and her father had named the car together.

Amanda turned onto the next road and made her way down the narrow two-lane road that led into the mountains. She had never been this way because her parents always went the long way around the mountains. They said they liked to take the scenic route.

She came to a small wooden sign that said *Slatesville—Welcome to your home away from home*. She smiled at the welcoming sign and kept on her way to the town. As she drove, she was amazed at how beautiful everything was. The low-hanging branches of the trees scraped the roof of the car every once in a while.

She was amazed at how many animals she saw. Deer acted as if they weren't afraid of her car. Raccoons were plentiful, and she jumped when a large black snake slithered across the road. There were people all around, and they watched her car curiously as she made her way down the street.

The town reminded her of a long lost western ghost town. It was a little spooky, and she caught herself checking the doors to make sure they were locked. The men nodded at her as she moved forward and many of the people smiled, although they held themselves back a little.

Amanda finally saw the sign that said *Montgomery Law Firm*. She pulled into one of the many vacant parking spots and slowly got out of the car. A handsome man leaned against the building she was about to enter. His brown eyes had flecks of yellow and orange in their deep depths. She smiled slightly, and the man just continued to stare as he looked her over slowly.

"Can I help you, ma'am?"

"I am just here to see Mr. Montgomery."

"Well, you're in the right place, Miss…?"

"Oh, Amanda. Amanda Walker. And you are?"

Something changed in his eyes as he smiled at her and made his way to her side. He held out his hand to her. "Name's Curtis Livingston."

"Oh. Do you live here?"

"Yes. I'm one of the controlling partners here in Slatesville. Well, I have to be going. It was good to meet you."

"You, too, Mr. Livingston."

"Please, call me Curt. Everyone does."

"Only if you call me Amanda."

"That's a deal, sweet lady." She flushed all over when he raised her hand to his lips and gently caressed her knuckles with a brief touch of his mouth. She felt the rise in temperature in her cheeks spread across her upper chest. She stood there and watched as he walked away from her down the street to slip inside a store. She felt foolish and realized that she had been staring. She shook her head, trying to think straight and clear the thoughts that were running through her mind.

Amanda was always aware that she wasn't the Barbie doll type of girl. Although she wasn't fat, she wasn't rail thin, which most men liked, either. Her waist and stomach didn't look like a washboard, although it didn't look like a bunch of bread dough either.

She instantly felt inadequate and quickly turned around to walk to the door of the attorney's office. Knocking, she was surprised when the door instantly opened. The man who opened the door wasn't what she expected. Mr. Montgomery was a short, pudgy man. He didn't wear a business suit, and he didn't seem stuffy at all. He was older and had a short goatee around his mouth. His hair was pulled back into a ponytail at the back of his neck, and he smiled when he saw her.

"You must be Amanda. You look just like your father, except for your eyes. You have your mother's eyes. Let's hope you didn't inherit your father's temper, though," he chuckled.

"You knew my father?"

"Oh, why yes, my dear. We grew up together, Josh and I. Have to say we got into a lot of trouble as kids, and your aunt Mabel was always there to wag her finger and tell on us. You see, there were the three of us; Joshua, Jeremiah, and I. We were called the three musketeers. Mabel wanted to be the fourth, but you know boys. We would never let her, so she always ran and told on us to get back at us for not including her; the little minx." He told the story fondly, and she instantly knew that this man held her family in the highest regard. She also knew he was her ticket to finding out the truth about her family.

"Do I have any more family that I don't know of?" She held her breath, as though she were a child again, asking if Santa Claus was real.

"I am sure you do, my dear. Unfortunately, your aunt was the last of your father's line. She couldn't have any children, and most of the family was killed in a fire in '90. I am sure there is still family on your mother's side, though. However, I must warn you that they are not the kind of people you want to know. Now, if you will come in, I will tell you about everything that now belongs to you."

"What?"

"Oh, my dear, you must know that your father's family had a legacy. You are the only Traverse left to take over the family business."

"What? I don't know what you're talking about."

"They never did tell you who you really are, did they? Oh, you poor child. I am afraid you are going to learn some things about yourself that are going to be hard for you. You must still be a virgin as well."

"I beg your pardon, sir, but I don't see how that's any of your damn business."

"No, my dear, I do not mean to be crude. I was just saying that you have never undergone the Change. It will happen, though. You recently turned twenty-four, and everything changes now."

"What change? What in the hell are you talking about?"

"They hid that from you, too? Oh my gosh. You don't know? Oh, Lord. Okay, first things first. You are now the owner of your family's estate."

"Family estate? So I have a house."

He smiled kindly at her. "Not just a house, my dear. It is what holds the legacy of your family name together. The estate has fifteen bedrooms with their own bathrooms and fireplaces, a kitchen, dining room, parlor, living area, office, library, Carolina room, staff quarters, wrap-around porch with two different sections screened in, pool, tennis courts and 300 acres. It was the pride and joy of your ancestor, Edgar. He was a distant grandfather of yours."

"Oh my gosh."

"Yes, ma'am. How about this? How about I get the keys and directions to the place? You go take a look at it, and then we can talk tomorrow about what you want to do. Stephan has been looking over things, and since your aunt's death, he has given everyone time off until you arrive and decide where to go from there."

Amanda wasn't sure she had the energy to deal with all of this tonight. "Unfortunately, it is very late. Is there somewhere that I can stay for a couple days and then I can go from there and take the day tomorrow to go look at the place?"

"That is perfect. Just give me a second, and I'll find a place for you to stay tonight."

Amanda sat quietly and listened to him talk on his phone. She didn't even hear his words as she thought of what she was going to do.

"I have gotten you a little cabin to rent down the road," he said, drawing her attention back to him. "It is in the woods a little but has electricity and such. On such short notice, I couldn't find anything else. It is only about ten minutes away. The key will be under the mat at the front door. Just go on in and make yourself at home."

"That is perfect. Thank you so much."

"You're welcome, my dear, and we will talk tomorrow. Say ten o'clock tomorrow morning? We will meet here and go to see the house together."

"Perfect. Thank you, Mr. Montgomery."

If you enjoyed this sample then look for **Romeo Alpha: A BBW Paranormal Shifter Romance - Book 1 by Darla Dunbar.**

Other Books by Carla Coxwell

- Torrid Exposure New Adult Romance Series

- Devil's Advocate BBW MC New Adult Romance Series

- Fifty Recipes For Disaster New Adult Romance Series

- Star Bright New Adult Romance Series

Get the latest update on new releases from the author at:

https://www.carlacoxwell.com/newsletter

About the Author - Carla Coxwell

Carla has always been a fan of romance novels. To augment what she made waiting on tables to help her way through college, Carla also did some freelance work in the romance genre.

Now she enjoys living vicariously through her characters in her New Adult Romance books.

Connect with Carla Coxwell

I really appreciate you reading my book! Here are my social media coordinates:

Friend me on Facebook:
https://www.facebook.com/CarlaCoxwell/

Follow me on Twitter: https://twitter.com/carlacoxwell

Check me out on Goodreads:
https://www.goodreads.com/author/show/10691544.Carla_Coxwell

Subscribe to my newsletter:
https://www.carlacoxwell.com/newsletter/

Visit my website: https://www.carlacoxwell.com/

www.ingramcontent.com/pod-product-compliance
Lightning Source LLC
Chambersburg PA
CBHW030817200726
48288CB00004B/1265